Age of Innocence

Age of Innocence

Book One of the Nia Trilogy Series

BY

Kimberly Purpoz

PUBLISHED BY MESSENGER BOOKS

A Division of Messenger Publishing, Incorporated

PRINTED IN THE UNITED STATES

Age of Innocence
Book One of the Nia Trilogy Series

ISBN: 978-0-9667913-9-6

Library of Congress Cataloging-in-Publication Data is
available upon request

Table of Contents

Chapter #1

Mama

Journal Entry #1

Dear God:

I am new to journal writing. So if I don't use proper English please forgive me Lord. Grandma Maria gave me this journal so that I can write down my deepest thoughts. She said it was a great way to talk to you, God. I want to share my feelings with you. And I want to do right by you because I want to go to heaven one day. Right now I am only fifteen years old but I have to grow up real fast.

I miss Grandma so much that it really hurts deep down inside. It's been three months since her death but my heart still yearns for her. Will this feeling of hurt ever go away or will it forever linger? God please bless me with a family and home.

Love,
Nia

September 1986

I can remember my younger years of growing up in Bronx, New York. It was 1986 and the colorful leaves were dancing gracefully along the sidewalk. Dark storm clouds began filling the sky and the cool breezy wind caused the trees to sway from side to side.

My name is Nia Yolanda Chavez. When I was fifteen years old, I was strolling through my neighborhood. I was coming from my best friend, Charlene's house in Castle Hill. Castle Hill is a mostly middle-class residential neighborhood located in the borough of the Bronx. The neighborhood has a high concentration of Latinos, a significant African American population and emerging pockets of West Indian immigrants.

My dark wavy hair was pulled into a long bushy ponytail and my luminous brown eyes reflected my youthfulness. Feeling chilly, I zipped up my jacket for warmth.

I reached the subway and got on the train, heading towards mama's house.

On the other side of the train, some teenage boys were listening to rap music on their boom boxes. They were talking so loud that I could hear their conversation from across the train.

The first teenage boy was dressed in a Starters jacket with a pair of Air Jordan's; his hair was cut in a box fade. The second teenager wore Reeboks sweat suit with a pair of Converse All Stars and his hair was in a Jerry Curl.

"Man I won that fuckin game fair and square. Did you see home boy blow up when he saw that we were winning?" The first teen put his boom box down.

"He and his hommies don't know what hit them when we beat them on the court!" The second teenager sat down and winked at me from across the aisle.

"What's up Shorty? How's my lovely, señorita? I would love having some Spanish flavor." I rolled my eyes because I was not at all interested. The second teenager sat down next to me and tried to continue to flirt with me. He placed his arms around my shoulder. I looked at him as if he had lost his freaking mind.

"Look I'm not your señorita! I do have a fuckin name." I gave him the brick wall and walked to the other side of the train.

"Ooh! Man you just got dissed!" The first teenager was cracking up laughing.

"Well forget you I didn't want you anyway!" The second teenager cursed and tried to play off his rejection.

I looked out the window. The train was going so fast that everything outside was just a blur. Eventually, the train made it to the next stop; there was graffiti all over the walls and trash everywhere.

I started daydreaming about my best friend Charlene. Charlene's father, Richard, was a Jamaican immigrant and her mother, Thelma, grew up in Queens, New York. They lived in the same building as my grandmother in Castle Hill. I remembered the time when I first met Charlene. The Thompson family moved into the building about three years ago.

Richard was a chef. He just finished up his culinary training and he opened up a Jamaican restaurant. And Charlene's mother was a receptionist at a law firm. She was going to school to become a paralegal.

My grandmother, Maria Chavez, had custody over me. Grandma Maria was a librarian; she retired about two years ago after working at the Bronx Library for over twenty years. About a year ago, Grandma was diagnosed with breast cancer. Doctors gave her chemotherapy treatment and did surgery, but the surgery was unsuccessful. The cancer spread throughout her body. I remembered how weak grandma was from the chemotherapy treatments. Grandma's hair fell out and she lost a lot of weight. I felt so sorry for grandma. And I did not know what I could do to make her feel better.

I can still remember the time when I found out about grandma's death. I called 911 when I could not revive her. The ambulance raced to Soundview Medical Center. The medical staff rushed her to the emergency room. I was not allowed to go in. "You will need to stay in the waiting room," said one of the doctors. I watched them roll grandma down the hall. I stood there and watched until they disappeared.

The waiting room was very cold. I felt so alone. I felt relieved when I saw Thelma. Thelma held me in a warm embrace, "Baby everything is going to be ok."

The doctors came to give us feed back on grandma's progress. The traumatic news of grandma's death echoed in my ears. "I am sorry but we could not save her. We did the best that we could but she did not make it." I felt like the walls were closing in on me because I literally felt like my world was turning upside down. I was stunned at first with disbelief. “She can’t be dead. She is all I got!” I wanted to see grandma. When I saw grandma’s lifeless corpse, I cried so hard in Thelma’s arms.

Grandma Maria died three months ago and I took it pretty hard. I was devastated because I did not know who was gonna take care of me. I knew I did not want to stay with mama, because she had some major issues of her own and this really saddened my spirit.

The train came to my stop and I got off. As I exited the subway, I looked around. The sky finally cleared up and I could see the stars shining so bright.

I saw homeless people laying in filthy alleys and sidewalks. Across the street, I saw a man exchanging money for drugs from a local drug dealer. I passed the park and saw some guys shooting hoops.

I reached the towering buildings of James Monroe Housing. I opened the door to my building and went up a flight of stairs.

When I got home I heard commotions going on inside mama’s apartment. From outside the door, I heard Rachel’s voice and a male’s voice yelling in the background.

I opened the door. Rachel was in the living room pleading with the local drug dealer name Q which was short for Quinton.

The living room had holes and stains all over the walls. Instead of having lovely curtains hanging in the windows, there were cheap floral sheets covering the window seals. On top of the battered wooden end table there was a picture of mama, during mama’s earlier years when she was not abusing drugs. In her pictures she was a beautiful woman, but years of street life was beginning to take hold on her body; her beauty was beginning to fade away.

“Rachael, where is my money?” Q cursed and grabbed her thin arms and shook her. He threw her on to the floor like a rag doll.

Mama was dressed in an extremely short, provocative, purple colored mini dress; her cleavage was showing. Mama’s once long silky shoulder length hair was now in disarray. Q was a chestnut complexion with gold streak in his hair. He had shaved line designs going through his hair and had the letter Q shaved into the back of his head. He had a gold herringbone necklace around his neck.

“Q, please-”

I closed the door and my heart was pounding as fast as a locomotive and my palms were clammy. I wanted to help mama but I knew it was too dangerous. He had a gun strapped to the back of his pants and he was known in the community for killing people with his street gang.

Rachael saw me standing by the door, Q's gaze followed Rachel's.

"Nia what are you doing here?" Rachel got up and adjusted her short dress.

"Mama-"

"Oh I see Rachael, you have a little girl. I didn't know that you have such a fine little thang. Maybe we can keep it all in the family." Q gave a sinister grin.

"Q, stay away from her your beef is with me!"

"I'm not going to give you anymore credits, Rachael!" Q turned around and approached mama.

"But there is one is thing you can do for me that would change my mind." Q took his long index finger and caressed her cleavage. His dark evil eyes stared into hers.

"Come on Q, my baby is here."

"You owe me! Don't make me cut you in front of your baby girl!" He cursed and glared into her eyes. He grabbed her arms real tight." Rachael winced in pain.

"Ok, Q But not out here."

"Baby, mama will be right back. This won't take long." Rachael blinked back her tears.

"Get your butt in here!" He cursed and smacked her hard on her bottom. He pushed her into the bedroom and slammed the door shut.

I sat in the living room and waited for mama. I could hear them moaning in the other room. I heard the head board from the bed banding against the wall. I shook my head in disgust.

Q opened the bedroom door. He adjusted his pants and had a dirty grin on his face.

Rachael's hair was puffy and in more disarray, she stepped out of the room and pulled down her dress and adjusted her dress straps.

"Here's ya damn drugs." Q threw the crack rocks on to the filthy floor."

Rachael plugged on to the floor in desperation. She was like a stray dog in the street foraging around trash cans for food.

Q shook his head, "You junky whore."

Q then turned his attention to me. I was sitting on the corner of the couch.

"You are a cute thang. I can have you walk the streets and sale your sweetness," he reached over and caressed my face. I turned my head away in disgust.

"You stay away from her! You got what you wanted now leave!" Rachael stood up.

"I'm leaving. I'll be over again for some repayment options. You still owe me." Q gave Rachael an insinuating look and winked. Rachael's eyes were filled with tears.

Rachael closed the door.

I rushed towards mama and hugged her.

"Mama you don't have to use those drugs. I miss you."

"I miss you too, baby."

"What are you doing here? You're supposed to be over Thelma's house."

"I know, but I wanted to see you, mama, and make sure you're ok."

"I'm fine."

Mama was sweaty and was beginning to tremble.

"What's wrong?"

"I need it baby."

"Look baby, I need you to leave it is not safe out here."

Rachael picked up her crack pipe and walked me towards the door.

"Now Nia, go back to Thelma's and stay there. My life is complicated right and I just don't need you in the middle of my mess." Rachael scratched her head in frustration.

"Ok mama."

Mama closed the door behind me.

Chapter #2

High School Blues

Journal Entry #5

Dear God,

School can be hard at times. I am not as smart as some of the other kids in my class. But my best friend Charlene has been helping me with my studies. I really love her and her family.

I am not sure what I want to do with my life but I know one thing for sure that I do not want to end up like mama. God please bless mama and help her to get better. I miss how things used to be between us.

Love,
Nia

October 1986

I was running towards my father. I was a little girl, about six years old. He had on his army uniform looking so tall, handsome, and strong. His name tag, read "Chavez". As we were just about to reach each other and he was ready to lift me into his arms, he vanished.

"Nia, Nia, Nia wake up girl! It's time to go; we got to get ready for school! Dang, girl, wake up!"

I rolled over and yawned.

"What time is it, Charlene?"

"Girl, it is going on 7:30, and we need to get up out of here. We have to be at school at 8:00!"

"OK."

"Hurry up. Don't, I have to leave your slow butt."

I crawled out of the bed and went to the bathroom. While brushing my long, thick, wavy hair, I couldn't get the dream off my mind. I often times wondered what daddy would have been like and if our lives would have been different if he had survived the war. Daddy was Puerto Rican. He was staff sergeant in the United States Army. He died in combat in 1970 during the Vietnam War, while mama was pregnant with me. I was getting tired of fooling with my hair so I pulled it back into a ponytail.

As soon as Charlene and I got dressed, we ran down the stairs. Hastily we grabbed granola bars. We made it to the subway.

While on the train we talked about cheerleading tryouts on Friday. We both said that we were going to try out for the cheerleading squad. We reached our stop. Charlene and I got off the subway and ran across the street to school.

The bell rang and we joined the crowd of students rushing into the school building.

The halls at Washington High School were dangerous due the street gangs in the neighborhood. The school installed metal detectors inside the buildings. The student body was mostly blacks and Hispanics.

It seemed like the day was lingering along in slow motion. It was time for lunch. Charlene and I met in the school cafeteria.

"So, girl, how are your classes so far?" a grin filled Charlene's pretty chocolate colored face.

"Oh, girl, please, school is school." I rolled my neck.

"Nia, you need to get serious about school. You know that, don't you?"

"Who cares?" I rolled my eyes and checking out my freshly filed fingernails.

"I care, Nia, and I want to go to college one day."

"Well, that's you, girlfriend." I started eating my cheeseburger and fries.

"Don't you want to go to college?" questioned Charlene with concern.

"Yeah, maybe one day, I just want to get up out of here."

"You will one day Nia, but now you need to get serious about the books."

"You're sounding like your mama."

"Yeah, and you know what? Mom is right."

"Well, I guess she is," I uttered.

"Personally, I think you should be more concerned about school because it can be your ticket out of the ghetto. Aren't you tired of the ghetto?"

"Yeah I am tired of it. I'm going to go somewhere, girl."

"Where are you going to go?"

"I'm gonna leave New York."

"Yeah, but if you don't get serious about your education, you ain't going nowhere!" Charlene rolled her neck and snapped her finger with an attitude.

"Oh come on Charlene, why don't you chill a little? Take a chill pill!"

"OK, Nia, I'm gonna lay off but for real you do need to take it seriously."

"I make C's."

"Yeah, and you also make D's. You need to pull up your grades."

I was getting very annoyed so I crossed my arms in front of my chest. Tears began to fill my eyes. What Charlene was telling me was hurting my feelings.

"Girl, I'm not trying to hurt your feelings, I'm being a friend and just being honest with you. You need to pull up your grades if you want to get somewhere in your life."

"I am going to get somewhere, I know I am," I mumbled.

I knew that Charlene was right, but it upset me to hear my best friend telling me that I was not doing my best. I knew Charlene was not trying to hurt me and that she was only trying to inspire me to do better.

After lunch, I went to my next class. What Charlene told me earlier had me really thinking about which direction I needed to take in school.

Maybe Charlene is right, maybe I do need to be more serious about my school work.

I'm young, I am fifteen years old, and I have plenty of time to think about my future. But, then again, I want to get up out of here. I don't want to be in the ghetto for the rest of my life. I want to be somebody. I want to make it, and I am going to make it, that's one thing for sure!

After school, Charlene and I met up to go to the cheerleading meeting. At the meeting, we found out when and where practice and tryouts were being held. The meeting only lasted for thirty minutes.

"Nia, are you going to make it to practice tomorrow?" asked Charlene.

"Yeah, I'm not going to miss this for nothing."

"Me either, girl. I'm going to be there."

"Well, I guess I better head on home then."

"Home?"

"Yeah."

"Are you coming over to my house tonight, Nia?" questioned Charlene.

"Um, I'm going to stop by my house first, to see how things are going. I need to check up on mama."

Charlene was about to say something but then she change her mind, so she said, "Never mind."

"No, Charlene. What were you going to say?"

"No, I think it's none of my business," stated Charlene, looking away.

"Girl, you are my best friend, and I want to know your opinion about things that are important in my life."

"I don't understand you," expressed Charlene, shaking her head with disapproval.

"What?"

"Your mom is up there using drugs. She doesn't know that you even exist. She could care less if you come home at night, and she doesn't even care about where you are. She doesn't give a damn about you, girl!"

I couldn't say a word because I knew that Charlene was right; all I could do was lower her head. My heart was telling me that I must go and see if mama was OK.

Charlene continued talking.

I looked at her and responded, "Because she is my mom, that's why."

"Nia, she's a junky that is what she is!"

"Come on, Charlene, that is my mom, and I care about her! I should really see how she is doing at least every once in a while."

"You know what? You should just come and stay with us always. You don't have to put up with all of that."

"I know, but I just want to see if she is OK."

"All right then, you can always come on over later."

"OK, thanks girl, I'll see you later." I gave Charlene a hug.

"OK."

I walked on home to the projects.

Down the street and I saw some girls playing Double Dutch near the fire hydrant.

A group of kids ran past me playing Hide-N-Seek. I sat down on a bench to watch. I saw a little boy, about seven years old. He closed his brown eyes and count while his friends ran to find hiding places.

The child yelled, "Ready or not, here I come!"

I smiled as I watched them play.

Across the street, I noticed that there were some people dealing drugs. I moved on along and saw people playing craps, gambling to rip each other off for money.

Some teens break dancing in the park. For a while, I stood and watched them dance. I even started to dance to the groove. The rap music was on, it was the kind of music that made people wants to get up and show off all their street moves.

I was having fun, but I knew it was time to move on. I passed a dirty local park with litter everywhere and graffiti on the walls. Some boys were playing basketball on the courts. Police sirens could be heard in the background.

I reached James Monroe Housing and I jogged up the flight of stairs. There was fowl language written along the dirty, filthy walls. On some of the steps, there were beer cans, cigarette butts, liquor bottles, and old news paper.

A huge obese rat ran right across of my path; I jumped because it scared the daylights out of me and frowned when I discovered it was only a rat. *Dang, this freaking place should be condemned.*

As I got to the top of the stairs, I saw my next-door neighbor, Fanny. Fanny sometimes hung out with mama. She was also a drug addict; she mainly shot up heroine.

"Hi, Fanny."

"Hi, how is it going?"

"Fine," I answered.

Fanny didn't look so hot. She still had rollers in her hair, her eyes had bags under them, and she had nothing on but her pink fuzzy robe.

I noticed Fanny appeared to be in a daze so I queried, "Are you OK?"

"Girl, I just need me a hit."

She came towards me and asked, "Do you have $10.00 I can borrow?"

"No, I don't," I responded.

"Well, don't you have any money I can borrow? I could surely use a dollar bill," she begged.

"No, I don't, Fanny. I just used my money on the subway." I took a step back.

I knew how drug addicts were; they would move closer to you to steal your wallet, so I knew to keep my distance. Fanny had the shakes and I knew she needed a hit for a quick fix.

"OK, then."

"I'll see you later."

"Bye," uttered Fanny.

I watched her as she walked away, and then turned around to unlock the door. I lied when I told Fanny I didn't have any money; I didn't feel like giving her dough for drugs. Drugs had destroyed Fanny and her family; not too long ago, a social worker had come and taken Fanny's children away from her because she was not taking good care of them. She was an unfit parent.

Well, here I am at my mama's house; I unlocked the door and walked on in.

"Mom, I'm home!"

I looked around and saw my mama.

"Oh, hi, dear. How are you doing?"

"I'm doing fine."

I smiled because I was so happy that mama did not seem to be high today. I hugged mama. Mama looked a little better than the last time I had seen her. Mama had a low cut top that showed her cleavage and a pair of tight jeans.

Mama stepped back to take a good look at me. Mama beamed, "You look so much like your father." Rachael had tears in her eyes. I studied mama's face and saw that she didn't look completely right; she was very skinny, and her eyes were red and had bags under them from using drugs.

I noticed that we were the same honey colored skin complexion and height, about five feet, three inches tall. Rachael was in the kitchen stirring some food in a bowl.

"What are you cooking?" I asked.

"Oh, I'm just fixing some tuna."

"Really?"

"Yeah."

Mama stood there with one hand on her slender hip and the other hand holding her cigarette. I watched her inhale and exhale. I saw the smoke from the cigarette silhouette into a gray cloud which eventually disappeared.

"So how was school today?"

"Oh, school was fine. School is school."

"Did you say hi to Quinton?"

"No, who is Quinton?"

"Oh you didn't meet him. Well he's in the living room, go say hi to him."

I peeked around the corner. Aw man, that's the same no good thug she had over last time, Quinton was actually Q, the gangster drug dealer. *Man, I didn't want to introduce myself.* Meanwhile, Rachael walked into the living room.

"Quinton, have you met my daughter?"

"No, I haven't met her and stop calling me Quinton, call me Q when you are around everyone else, bitch!" he snapped in agitation. He grabbed mama's arm really tight. Rachael's smile faded away. Her faced was filled with fear.

"Well here she is. This is my little girl, Nia." Rachael blinked back her tears and rubbed her arms when he finally let go.

She spun around and saw Nia still standing in the kitchen peeking around the corner. Looking angrily, Rachael shoved me over to where Q was standing.

"Say hi to him girl, now don't you try to act all shy!" demanded Rachael.

I already knew that I despised him, so I rolled my eyes at him and said, "Hi."

Q casually eyed me up and down. His eyes were glued to my breasts. I was well developed for a fifteen year old girl.

He stared boldly into my eyes and said, "Hi, it's nice to meet you."

"It's nice to meet you, too," I mumbled as I distastefully shook his hand.

I felt very uncomfortable around him. I noticed the gold in his mouth. I glanced at his hands; they were very big and crusty looking.

I saw the gold streak in his hair. His dark eyes stared boldly into mines. He was much larger than I was. I had to look up to him. He towered over me. Q was solid with muscles. I could smell alcohol under his breath. I couldn't understand what her mama saw in this man.

I walked away from both of them and turned on the TV to watch *The Jeffersons*. I was cracking up over George and Florence because they kept on joning each other. Suddenly a wave of uneasiness came over me; I felt someone watching me. I turned around and discovered that Q was staring at me. Lust was all over his face. His eyes were piercing with fire, as he licked his lips. I watched his hands go down to his crotch. He began to fondle himself. I turned around in repulse; I knew that Q was definitely a sick man.

I shot out of the room; his presence made me feel scared and unsafe. Q started snickering. In his wicked train of thought, he picked up his 'forty' and took another swig.

I went to the kitchen.

"So Nia, are you going to stay here today?" Rachael asked.

I hesitated a little and said, "I might stay here, I don't know."

"Do you want some tuna?" asked Rachael, cutting her tuna sandwich in half. I looked around and saw roaches crawling everywhere, crumbs all over the counter, and dirty dishes scattered all over the kitchen.

"I don't think so Mom," I answered politely.

The whole place was in shambles. I used to try to keep the apartment clean, but by the time I finished cleaning up, mama and her crackhead friends would have everything messed up again. I felt that there was no point in cleaning up anymore, so I just let it be.

After Rachael finished eating her tuna sandwich, she picked up her crack pipe. I became teary eyed; I didn't want to see mama getting high again.

"Mom, do you really want to do that right now? Can't we just sit down and talk?"

With frustration in her voice, Rachael asked, "Nia, what is there to talk about?"

"We never talk like we used to. Do you remember the times we spent together, just you and me? You used to work those two jobs, and we lived in an apartment on the other side of town. Do you remember those days, Mama? I loved those days, Mama." I spoke fast, hoping to start a nice, long, warm conversation with mama for a change.

Angrily Rachael answered, "Yeah, I remember those days too, but do you remember when we were thrown out, evicted, and homeless?"

"Yeah, I remember that too, Mom. But, at least, we had each other. Why can't things be like they were?"

Rachael gently cupped my face with her hands and responded, "Honey, time moves on, remember that. I like this drug. I need it. It's the only way I can survive."

"Mom, I'm losing you. You're not the same," I cried as I held mom's hands.

"Darling, it might not ever be the same."

Rachael lit a match and inhaled the smoke from her pipe. Rachael was gone, gone off into her own little world. And Q was still sitting on the couch drinking his 'forty'. He had his feet propped up on the old dusty coffee table.

I wept. Mama didn't want to sit down and have a mother and daughter talk with me. Man, my own mom never even told me about the birds and the bees. Mrs. Thompson was the one who spoke to me about sex. Every time I went home, I always ended up disappointed and depressed; it seemed like mama was pushing me away and didn't want to be bothered. *Maybe Charlene was right about mama it just seemed like she does not give a damn about me.*

I might as well call the Thompson my family; I felt more at home at their house than I did at my own. It was a tragic feeling to know that I was losing mama to drugs.

I went back to the Thompson's house. I made up my mind that I was not going over to mama's house anymore. I figured that mama had Mrs. Thompson's phone number so she knew how to reach me.

I reached the Thompson' and rung the doorbell. Thelma opened the door with a warm smile and a hug.

I was about to ask her if she could stay over when Mrs. Thompson interrupted me by saying, "Girl you come right on in here!" She opened the door wide to let me in. "You don't have to ask me just come right on in; you're a part of this family."

"Thanks," I smiled.

I went upstairs to Charlene's room. I put my things down on one of the twin sized beds and went back downstairs. I washed my hands and went into the kitchen to help Mrs. Thompson chop up lettuce for the salad.

"So, how was it seeing your mama?"

"It was OK," I replied with lack of enthusiasm.

"Is she still using that stuff?"

"Yeah, but at least this time she was not high when I first saw her."

"That's good. Did you get a chance to talk to her for a while?"

"Yeah a little bit, for a little while. She had this man over, and I don't like him." I frowned as I thought of Q

"Yeah, doesn't she always do?" Thelma rolled her eyes as she thought about the negativity going in and out of Rachael's apartment."

"I'm glad you let me stay over here, Mrs. Thompson, this is the place I can truly call home." My eyes filled with love for this dear person.

"Nia, you do have a place to call home. You can call this your home. Nia, you're a good kid, you remember that," said Thelma, while cooking.

I beamed, because I haven't heard a good word about myself in a long time. The compliment made me feel mellow deep inside.

I always heard negative things from mama. Mom always told me that I was nothing, that I would never amount to anything, and that I would always be nothing. Hearing this compliment from Thelma made me feel stronger and more confident. I reached over and hugged Thelma, Thelma hugged me back.

After I finished helping with dinner, I went upstairs. That night I actually sat down and did my homework. I haven't done that in a long time; for a change, I really studied.

Chapter #3

Crush

Journal Entry # 16

Dear God,

This week is cheerleading try outs. I am looking forward to trying out for the cheerleading squad.

I am enjoying my stay at the Thompson's house. I want to thank you God, for having the Thompson family in my life. Without them I would probably be out in the streets by now turning tricks and using drugs just like mama. I am thankful that I have a place to call home.

Love,
Nia

October 1986

The colorful autumn leaves filled the campus trees and landed gracefully upon the school grounds. It was Friday, the day of cheerleading tryouts. We were getting ready in the girls' locker room. I was excited but nervous at the same time.

We left the locker room and went into the gym. Coach Williams called out everyone's name in ABC order. I was one of the first to perform.

I went to the middle of the gym floor and began my routine. My heart was beating as fast as a locomotive, my stomach had butterflies, and the palms of my hands were sweaty.

I included flips, cartwheels, splits, and enthusiasm in my cheer. When I was done, and I stood before the judges for a brief moment. It seemed like an eternity. Coach finally told me that I could sit down.

I felt relieved and proud of myself; I knew that I have given it my best shot. Charlene moved to where I was sitting.

"You did great," whispered Charlene.

"You really think so?"

"I know so. You did your routine perfectly. They're gonna choose you."

"Yeah, I hope you're right."

Meanwhile, Coach had called almost everyone's name on the list. I noticed that Charlene was chewing her nails; whenever she was nervous, she would always chew on her fingernails like a squirrel nibbling on an acorn.

It was Charlene's turn. She walked to the middle of the gym floor to begin her routine.

I keenly observed Charlene as she did her cheers. Charlene did everything she was supposed to do. She did an excellent job.

"How did I do?" asked Charlene.

"I think you did great," I whispered.

After the tryouts were over, Coach Williams stood before the girls and gave a brief speech.

"Well girls, all of you did a wonderful job. Now we are going to ask you to take a fifteen minute break, to get a soda or whatever snack you want and come right back. During the break, the judges will be calculating the scores and decide on who made the team."

Coach Williams walked away swiftly.

"That Coach Williams is a trip," I remarked with a smirk.

"Yeah, she is," agreed Charlene.

"She always have her nose up in the air, talking like she's all that!" I exclaimed.

"Yep," laughed Charlene.

“Hey, I’m Ms. Williams, I’m Coach Williams,” I began mocking Coach with my nose in the air and my hands on my hips.

“Girl, you are crazy, you are up here mocking her,” laughed Charlene.

“Yeah, but she does talk like that and have her nose way up in the air.” I had a silly expression on my face.

“You need to stop mocking her,” added Charlene, trying to keep a straight face.

“Girl, you know that it is funny,” I laughed.

Charlene started laughing so hard that tears began to roll down her cheeks.

“Girl, you’re so silly,” chortled Charlene trying to catch her breath.

During our break, Charlene and I went downstairs to the vending machine. I had a Snickers bar and a Coke Cola, and Charlene bought herself a bag of Doritos and a Sprite. We sat at one of the tables located near the snack bar.

“All right, cross your fingers,” said Charlene.

“I’m going to cross mines.” Charlene was really munching on her Doritos like they were going out of style.

“Man, it would be so smooth if we get to wear those uniforms and go to every basketball game. We can really check out all those fine boys,” said Charlene.

Charlene can really talk fast and put so many words together in one combined sentence. Most people have to tell her to slow down, but fortunately, I understood every word she said.

“Girl, you are boy crazy,” I laughed.

“You are too, Nia. You know that you look at all those guys.”

“Yeah, I know.”

Out of the blue, a good looking guy walked down the hall.

“Wait a minute; did you see that boy right there?” I pointed my index finger in the direction the cute guy was walking.

“What boy?”

“That boy that just—come on, lets get up and find him!” I reached over and playfully pulled Charlene out of her seat.

“Girl, you are crazy, why are you going to follow this guy?”

“I am following him because he is F-I-N-E, fine!”

We rushed to try to find the handsome stud.

My heart was beating fast. For some reason, I knew that I had to meet this guy.

"Girlfriend, are you insane? You don't even know this guy!" exclaimed Charlene.

"And you had the nerve to call me boy-crazy! At least I'm not the one running up and down the school halls trying to find this big hunk!"

As I peeked around the corner, I spotted him.

"Come here, Charlene, there he is," I whispered. We both took a peek at Mr. Good Looking himself.

"Oh, that boy is fine."

"Shh, shh, he might hear us."

He stood at his locker taking out some books and putting them inside his book bag. He was very tall, perhaps six feet tall, with a medium brown complexion. He also had a cute fuzzy mustache, I observed. The guy had on a blue Washington High basketball jersey, black sweat pants and a pair of black Nike basketball high tops.

"Do you know him?" I asked.

"No, I don't know him."

"Hmm...He must be a junior or a senior, then."

I wondered who he was; I rubbed my chin, plotting about how I was going to get this guy to notice me without looking like a complete fool.

"He might be a senior. Um, I wouldn't mind meeting him," I admitted.

"Why don't you go up to him, girl?"

"Nah, he might not like me, and I don't want to look too obvious."

"How do you know if he doesn't? Why don't you just say 'hi' and introduce yourself?"

"Nah, I don't think I should do that."

"Nia, you acting all shy! Just go up to the boy, he's only a human being."

"That's easy for you to say, Charlene! You can't even go up and talk to that boy name Scott you like so much because every time you see him you, drool."

"Now, Nia, that's a different story," said Charlene folding her arms across her chest.

"How is that different?"

"It's different because Scott is drop dead gorgeous and superfine and I ain't going near him."

"Girl, you know that you like Scott, and you should try to talk to him."

"What are you trying to do, Nia? Are you trying to keep yourself from approaching this guy or what?" Charlene could see right through my little scheme of trying to change the subject.

"You must be scared, Nia."

"Yeah, I'm afraid. What if he turns me down, and what if he doesn't like me?"

I paused for a moment. Suddenly I came up with a neat idea.

"Maybe if I walk by and smile, maybe I can get his attention."

I looked around the corner and noticed that home boy was walking away from his locker and starting up the steps.

"Oooh, girl, we got to catch up! He's going up the steps!"

Running side-by-side, we fled up the steps after the guy.

At the top of the staircase, the mysterious guy was talking to another boy who was also wearing a basketball jersey. They must be going to basketball practice, I speculated.

"Maybe if I walk on by them, he would look at me."

"You could try it."

I made up my mind to stroll by them. I walked on by him slowly with a casual but seductive stride; I looked at him, hoping that he would notice me. At last, he looked up and saw me. We made instant eye contact; he smiled first, and then I smiled back.

After I passed by them, he grinned and asked his friend Marcus, "Hey, man, did you see that cute girl that just walked past us?"

"Yeah, she's fine."

"Do you know her, man?"

"Naw, I don't think I know her, but I have seen her before. I think she's in the eleventh grade."

"Man, she is fine!" Clay turned his head as he watched me going down the hall and down the steps. He grinned at what just took place.

"He noticed me, he noticed me, he noticed me, girl!" I shouted.

"You're so silly," uttered Charlene.

I kept on bouncing around, "He even smiled at me, girl."

"I saw it, he smiled."

"And I smiled back. Maybe he does like me."

"Yes, he smiled but that does not mean anything. Just take it one step at a time and don't rush things."

"OK, OK, OK, but he is cute!"

"Yeah, I have to admit he is cute," smiled Charlene.

"Well, our fifteen minutes are up, and we need to go back downstairs to see if we made it." Charlene glanced down at her watch.

"OK."

We ran down the steps and reached the gym. The judges were still calculating the score.

"Gosh, they're not finished yet. We could have stayed upstairs and kept on flirting."

"Girl, you are crazy!"

"And you are, too." We giggled.

"If Scott was up there you would be drooling."

"Yeah, you ain't joking about that."

"And I know that for a fact."

Moments later, Coach announced who had made the cheerleading squad.

"Well, girls, we have the list of who made the squad. For those who didn't make it, we are glad that you have at least tried..."

Yeah, yeah, yeah, just call out the names.

Coach continued to talk, "...And we ask you to do try again, because next time you might make it. For those who did make the squad, congratulations. All right then."

It's about time she stopped yapping that mouth of hers.

Finally, Coach Williams called out the names.

"Amy Adams." Amy was jumping up and down with joy.

"Brenda Garcia."

Dang, I wish she would call out my name.

Coach called some more names and then some more names. My stomach was filled with butterflies.

Then, I heard Charlene's name.

"Charlene Thompson."

I reached over and hugged Charlene.

"Gosh, I made it!" beamed Charlene.

Dang, she called everybody's name except mines. I sighed. Tears began to fill my lovely almond-shaped brown eyes.

"The last person is Nia Chavez." I sighed with relief; hearing my name was like music to my ears.

Charlene and I hugged each other and screamed, jumping up and down. Instead of going straight home, we decided to stop by the ice cream parlor to celebrate by ordering banana splits.

We sat down and dove into the sticky sweetness. While we were eating, Scott walked in the door. Charlene looked in disbelief, "Nia is that who I think it is?"

I turned around and nodded, "Yeah, girl that is?"

"Charlene, he's all right, so what if he's the star football player."

"He's such a dream." Charlene stared at him from across the parlor.

I turned back around and saw him standing near the cash register to place his order. I still couldn't understand what Charlene thought was so great about him. Maybe it was because he was a red bone, Charlene had a thang for light skinned guys.

"Girlfriend, he looks OK. He ain't all that," I stated bluntly.

"Look at his caramel colored skin and those rippling muscles."

"Girl, why don't you just go up there?"

"No way, I can't do it."

"Why don't you say 'hi' or do what I did and walk by him and smile, maybe he would notice you then."

"I can't do that," whimpered Charlene, shaking her head no.

Charlene was a very pretty girl. She had lovely, smooth, rich chocolate colored skin. Her hair was jet black, shoulder length, silky in texture. She kept her hair in a mushroom type style, popular at the time. Her stunning, sparkling, brown eyes were wide with a touch of innocence. And she had soft chubby cheeks and a very cute button nose.

With her looks, Charlene could practically get any guy she wanted I thought. A lot of the boys liked her, but unfortunately, Charlene had a thang for older guys; she always said that older guys were more mature than the ones her age and that is why she always chased after them.

"Charlene, you are pretty, just go over there and smile."

Instantly, a very nice looking girl walked in. She was very busty, her breast were the size of melons. Miranda had on a pair of skin tight Jordache jeans. She was a fair, medium brown complexion. Miranda had charming hazel colored eyes that most girls only dream of having.

She spotted Scott and walked towards his table with a very seductive smile on her face. She placed her arms around him and gave him a kiss on the cheek.

"Miranda, Miranda, why she always has to come up and ruin everything?" mumbled Charlene.

"Well, she's not called Fast Miranda for nothing," I added while rolling my eyes.

"You know there's a bad rumor going around school about her, and most people think she's a whore," I said.

"I know she's fast. She's Miss Hot Thang, look at that skimpy outfit she has on...her blouse is too low cut and shows off everything. And look at Scott, he's drooling and can't keep his eyes off her. Man, no telling what they're going to be doing tonight," uttered Charlene in disgust.

"Well, maybe you didn't need him in the first place," I said.

"Maybe I don't need him because I heard that he's a dog anyway!"

"Yeah, you don't need a dog, Charlene. You know, there are better guys and other fish in the sea," I smiled wisely.

"Yeah, you're right, girl. I just wish he knew I exist, though." Charlene began to mope.

"He's not going to notice a nice girl like you. He's a senior and he probably only date's fast girls or other girls in the 12th grade.

"But Miranda is just in the 11th grade just like us."

"Oh, yeah, but she has a bad reputation. Guys tend to like those types of girls."

"Yeah, but one day," muttered Charlene, in a daze.

We eventually left the ice cream parlor and went home. I didn't even bother to go back by to tell mama the good news. I knew mama wouldn't care that I had made the cheerleading squad. For a whole week, I did not return home; I didn't have anything to say to mama anymore. I felt that there was no point in going back; my real home was with the Thompsons.

When we got home, we told Thelma the outstanding news about making the cheerleading squad.

"Girls, you all really made the team?"

"Yes, we did, Mom," Charlene smiled.

“That’s great! We’re going to celebrate this special occasion. I’m going to take you all out to get some pizza.” Mrs. Thompson hugged both of us.

Charlene and I were very excited about going out for pizza. We didn’t even mind that Charlene’s little brother, Joseph, also tagged along. It was the end of a very exciting day.

Chapter#4

Perverted Thug

Journal Entry #24

Dear God,

I am trying to be a good girl and do the right things. I am trying to look out for mama but it is hard. I am only fifteen years old and I should not have to try to look out for mama. It should be the other way around.

I am tired Lord. God if you can hear me. Please save mama. I already lost grandma and I can't stand to see mama going astray.

Love,
Nia

November 1986

The season of the year gradually changed. The brightly colored leaves gently dropped from the trees. And the trees were getting bare for winter.

It has been two months since I have last seen mama. Today I decided to go visit her.

"So, Nia did you change your mind about going over to your mom's house?"

"No, Charlene, I think today I should go see her."

"Yeah, I guess I have to agree with you. You haven't been over there in a long time."

"I know I can't stay mad at my mama forever."

"Yeah, girl, you can't be."

"Well, are you going to be back in time for the basketball game?"

"Yeah, I am. I'm going to walk to my mom's house, and then I'll head back to school," I added with a puzzled look on my face.

"Are you OK?"

"Yeah, I'm fine."

"Are you going to spend the night?"

"Yeah, I'm going to spend the night."

"OK, then I'll see you later."

"Bye."

We waved to each other and went our separate ways.

I walked over to mama's house. I had on my thick overcoat, boots, and gloves. The snow was continuously falling from the sky; I wrapped my scarf even tighter around my neck. My nose and ears were very cold from the brisk wind. *Gosh, wouldn't it be nice to have some earmuffs on right about now?* I pulled my scarf over my mouth in an effort to keep warm.

Being a native New Yorker, I was pretty much accustomed to the cold weather of Bronx, New York. There were a lot of people on the road, even though it was snowing. I literally cracked up when Charlene told me about how people in Georgia don't even go to school when it sleets, drizzles, or snow, even a little bit. *Man, the snow down there is a joke compared to the snow we get up here*.

I looked across the street and I saw the same guy that she had seen in school a while back, the cute guy that I followed around school with Charlene. *Dang, he's so fine. I wonder what his name is.* I watched the mystery guy stroll down the street with his friends until they could no longer be seen through the falling snow.

I kept on walking through the softly falling flakes. A million thoughts were crossing though my mind all at once. I reached my building at James Monroe Housing and went up the flight of stairs. The walls were still dirty and the place was still infested with rats and roaches. Nothing seemed to have changed.

I unlocked the door.

"Mama!" I yelled. There was no response.

Dang, Mom must not be home. Where she is? I looked around to see if anyone was there, and then sat down at the kitchen table to wait. Moments later, someone opened the door. It was Rachael.

"Hi, Mom."

"Hi."

"I haven't seen or heard from you in a while."

"I know."

"So, how are you doing?" I waited for mama to look my way. Rachael hung up her coat and then came into the kitchen.

"I'm fine," sighed Rachael.

It took her a long time to respond to my question. Mama turned around and she had a black eye!

"Who's been hitting you?" I cried.

I went to the refrigerator and got some ice to put in a plastic bag.

"Oh, nobody." Rachael looked away.

"What's going on Mom? I haven't heard from you in a while and now, this..."

I approached mama and placed the ice bag over her eye. I could see that mama was nervous and scared about something. She wouldn't look me straight in the face.

"I can't call you, of course, because the phone has been disconnected. But, Mom, what's going on?" I questioned her once again, as I held her hand.

"Well, do you know that guy that was over here a while back?"

"Oh, that gansta, thug, Q?"

"Don't call him a thug, dear."

Well, he is a thug and a crazy one too, if I may add.

"Is he your boyfriend?"

"Yeah, he was, but I have some good news, dear," smiled Rachael.

"What is it, Mom?"

You broke up and will never see each other again.

"Q and I just got married," replied Rachael. A big grin spread across her haggard face.

Hearing the bad news made my heart sank.

"Married! What do you mean, you two got married!" I yelled.

"We just got married at the court house, and we want you to stay with us. Q and I talked about this the other night."

"What?" I said, unbelievingly. The idea of staying with mama and Q made me nauseous.

"I don't want you staying with Thelma anymore!" snapped Rachael.

"But I love it there. I like staying at Charlene's house!"

"Well, I can understand that, but we still want you to stay here with us. This is your home, and you shouldn't be over there all the time!"

"But, Mom-" I was close to crying.

"No, listen, dear! Listen to me! We're you parents now, Q and I. And we want you to stay here with us. OK, and that's final! You're going to stay with us, and there's no questions asked, all right!" Rachael yelled angrily, pointing her finger in my face.

Can't Mom see how she's shattering my world? Doesn't she care? I just can't stay here; it would be like living in hell.

"But Mom-!"

Mama interrupted again, "Nia, I don't want to hear it!"

She folded her thin arms across her small breasts and said, "I want you to get your stuff from over there and bring it over here, because you're going to stay here with us from now on. And anyway, I miss you."

Mama reached out her slender arms to me. I walked over and hugged her.

"I miss you too, Mom."

But, Mom you're a drug addict, you don't act like a mother, you always get high, and I never have a chance to talk to you.

I wanted to tell mama my thoughts, but I didn't dare.

"Anyway, Q should be up here in a minute," said Rachael

"What happen to your eye?" I queried.

Rachael gently touched my shoulder and said, "Oh dear, don't worry about that."

He must have done it!

Q finally walked through the door.

"So did you tell her the news?" he asked in a deep thunderous voice.

"Yeah, I told her," said Rachael giving him a long passionate hug.

"Nia, go give your new father a hug!" demanded Rachael.

"Aw, Mom!"

I didn't want to go anywhere near that nasty pervert. I hated him with a passion.

"Do it now!" yelled Rachael with her hands on her hips.

Rachael walked out and went into the bathroom. Nia looked at Q with a hateful glance.

"Give your daddy a hug," said Q with a crooked smile on his face.

He towered over me. I hated looking into his dark ice cold eyes. I didn't want to hug him, but I didn't want to hear mama's mouth later on.

I was about to hug him when he snatched me into his arms. I could smell the fowl scent of alcohol under his breath. He started fondling me. I tried to push him away, but he overpowered me.

The whole ordeal was like a game to him.

"Stop it!" I yelled. I couldn't believe what was happening to me.

"Come here, girl," said Q I kept on trying to break away from his forceful grip.

"Please, stop it!" I yelled once again.

He started laughing at me. I began to cry.

I continuously tried to push him away, screaming, and "Let me go!"

He whispered, "You might as well get use to this, Nia, and try to start enjoying it because-."

Q let me go when he heard Rachael coming out of the bathroom.

"You know your mom said that you are going to stay here, don't you?"

Q had a sinister look on his face. I knew that I was in danger when I was near this man, and the thought frightened me greatly.

How could she leave me here alone and unprotected with this horrible man?

"Yeah, she did," I answered.

He winked at me and he moved a little closer. I moved away from him and stood closer mama.

The thought of him touching me and winking at me made me physically ill. I had to leave.

"Mom, I am going to the basketball game."

"OK, you be back with your things, now. From now on, you're going to be staying with us," slurred Rachael.

"All right," I bite my bottom lips. I had no intentions on coming back home.

I could feel Q's evil eyes staring at me.

"I'll see you later, dear. Come give your mom a hug," slurred Rachael. I hugged mama and kissed her on the cheek.

I looked at her mama. "Are you sure you're all right?"

"Yeah, I'm fine."

I was about to walk out the door.

"Oh you are going to walk by me and not give me a hug?" Q asked sarcastically. I looked at him like he was crazy and rushed out the door.

Chapter #5

Sistas

Journal Entry #35

Dear God,

I am very scared. Q has been eyeing me and making me feel uncomfortable. I don't like visiting mama any more especially since she is married to him. He is always there all of the time.

God, Q has already violated me and I don't feel safe. Please God don't make me live with them. Please let me continue to live with the Thompson family.

Love,
Nia

I didn't want to stay with her mama, especially since Q would be living there. If I'm ever left alone with this man, I feared that he would rape me.

I have to do what mama says because she is my mom. I have to talk to someone about this, perhaps Charlene; I can't handle this alone it's just too much for me to bare.

My long brisk walk was a blur. My mind was consumed by troubled thoughts. I don't even recall me getting on the train and getting off my stop.

When I reached school, I spotted Charlene standing inside the front entrance.

"Hi, girl, how are you doing?" asked Charlene. A warm smile came across her cute face.

"Oh, I'm fine," I mumbled.

"Why are you looking so down and gloomy?" She placed a caring hand upon my shoulder.

"Girl, it's a long story."

"Really?" Charlene put her coat on.

"Yeah."

"Well we have about two hours before the game starts. Do you want to go to the subway shop, eat, and talk about this some more?"

"Sure."

"Let's go."

We reached the sub shop.

"Do you have any money?" asked Charlene.

"Oh, no, I don't have any money," I answered.

"Well, Mom gave me some extra money just in case you did not have any." Charlene reached inside her purse and pulled out a ten dollar bill and handed it to me.

"Your mom is so sweet."

"Yeah, she figured that you wouldn't have any spending money, so she told me to give you some."

"Aw, tell her thanks for me," I said.

"What you mean, you can tell her tonight." Charlene had a crossed look on her face.

"I don't know if I'll be able to stay."

"Why?" Charlene asked curiously.

"That's part of the long story I have to tell you."

"Oh, OK, we can talk about it over our sub sandwiches, then."

While in line placing our orders, we talked about various things, mainly boys.

"So, have you seen Scott?"

"Oh, yeah, I saw him going down the hall at school with Miranda," answered Charlene.

"Oh, really?"

"Yeah he was still with that same girl we saw at the ice cream parlor a while back," answered Charlene.

"Well, maybe one day he will notice you, Charlene."

"Yeah, right, I don't think that he will ever know that I exist."

"What about you and that mystery guy, Nia?"

"Oh, yeah, that's one of the things that I wanted to talk to you about. Girl, I saw him today," I smiled.

"You did?"

"Yeah, I saw him when I was walking home. He was walking the other direction with his hommies."

"Oh, really?"

"Yes, he looked so good, and I still don't even know his name."

"Why don't you go up to him and ask him his name?"

"Nah, I can't do that, I'm waiting for him to approach me first."

"Well, you may be waiting forever for him to approach you, girlfriend."

"That's true," I admitted.

"Isn't he going to play at the basketball game?"

"I hope so." I did recall seeing him in a basketball jersey.

We sat in a booth across from each other.

"Hmmm, this food smells good," said Charlene, sniffing the appetizing aroma.

"I'm hungry," I added.

"So what do you have to tell me?" queried Charlene, with a raised eyebrow.

"Girl, it's awful," I answered sadly. My eyes became watery when I thought of going back home to mama.

"Charlene, my mom wants me to move back in with her."

"What?"

"Isn't that awful?"

"Yes, it is. I can't believe this! Why does she want you to stay with her after she's been dissing you? She's not much of a mama! Girl, I wouldn't go back if I was you," snapped Charlene, shaking her head with disapproval.

"Not only that, Charlene, she married that man."

"What man?"

"You know that man I told you about, the gansta thug, Q"

"Yeah."

"Well, they got married," I added.

"No!" exclaimed Charlene. Her mouth flew open and her eyes widened in shock.

"Yes, girl, they went to city hall and got married."

"Gosh, that's a real bummer."

"And not only that, Charlene, I can't trust this man."

"Really?"

Charlene took another sip of her soda.

"Why can't you trust him?" she asked.

I looked down and started to cry. Charlene moved to the other side of the booth to sit next to me. She put her arms around me to comfort me. She gave me a napkin to wipe my tears.

"Why are you crying? This must be horrible!" queried Charlene.

I began to tremble.

"I'm scared, Charlene."

"Why are you scared, Nia?" asked Charlene with deep concern.

"Because I think he beats on my mama."

"Really, did your mother tell you that?"

"No, but she had a black eye, and I believe he did it," I answered. I took another sip of my soda.

"How do you know if a drug dealer didn't do that?" asked Charlene.

I knew why Charlene asked that question. About three months before, another drug dealer beat up mama because she didn't have the money to pay him back for drugs she had bought on credit.

"I think that this time it's different, and I believe that he beats on her, I really do."

"Gosh," said Charlene.

"And not only that, Charlene, when I went to hug Q, he felt on me," I cried.

"He violated you, girl?" questioned Charlene. She covered her mouth in shock.

"He was feeling up on me."

"He did what? But that's molestation. Girl, you're only fifteen years old," whispered Charlene.

"I know," I agreed.

"Man, it would be different if he was your boyfriend, but this man is old. He is your step father. He shouldn't be doing this. And most of all, you should be able to trust him!"

"I know I shouldn't move back in with her, but I don't have much of a choice. Mama wants me to come back, and she has custody over me. Oh, I don't want to go back, Charlene!"

"I don't blame you. You got to find a way out of this, girl. You can't stay there."

"I know," I admitted sadly.

"Gosh, if that man was sick enough to do that, no telling what else he might do."

"I know, and that's why I'm so scared. If I move back home, I'm afraid he might rape me."

"If I was you, I would stay away. Who knows? She'll probably be stoned tonight, so she most likely won't know if you went home or not."

"Yep, she's probably high right about now," I added. I stared off in a daze for a second.

"Is she still skinny, Nia?" asked Charlene.

"Yeah, she is as skinny as a rail, and she looks terrible."

"Girl, you can always come and stay with us anytime. You know that my mom always tells you that you have a home with us." Charlene gave me a loving hug.

"Nia it will be all right, everything will be fine, so perk up a little. If you are scared, you don't have to go stay with your mom. That's a sick old man, and he knew exactly what he was doing. Maybe we should tell my mother about this."

"No, no, please don't tell your mother," I said quickly. I was very embarrassed about the whole situation and didn't want anyone else to know about it.

"Why don't you want my mom to know about this?" asked Charlene.

"I just don't. I really don't think it's a good idea," I answered.

"Well, Nia, what are you going to do?"

"I don't know. I'm going to try my best to stay with you all. I like it over at your house. I feel like a part of the family." I wiped the tears from my eyes with my napkin.

Charlene moved back to her side of the table. "Dang, girl, you have it bad."

"I know, but I'm going to figure something out. I'm not going to let this get me down," I added.

"I hope things work out for you," added Charlene, finishing up her sub-sandwich.

There was a moment of silence.

"Girl, let's perk up, let's talk about something else," mumbled Charlene.

"Yeah let's talk about something else," I agreed.

I knew that my eyes were red from crying so hard; I was glad I have a close friend to talk to.

"Yeah, now tell me about that guy you saw walking down the street."

"Yeah, girl, he looked so good. He's so fine and bow legged. I might try to approach him one day."

"Yeah, you should," added Charlene.

Charlene looked at my plate.

"Well I'm finished with my sandwich. You didn't eat much of yours, you barely put a dent in it." Charlene casually observed my plate.

"I'm not hungry."

"Our earlier conversation must have made you lose your appetite."

"Yeah, it did," I shrugged my shoulders.

"Don't worry, girl, things will get better for you."

"Yeah, I hope so. God is right by my side, and he will pull me through."

Charlene glanced at her watch and said, "Well, I guess we better go, it's already 6:00 pm. We're supposed to be at the gym by 6:30 pm."

Charlene and I left the submarine-shop. We walked back to the school together, each in complete harmony with the other. We came from two completely different worlds and, yet, we still managed to stay best friends.

This time, things seemed a little different. Charlene now held a deep dark secret that I shared with her. Knowing this secret and sharing my pain made Charlene feel like more than my best friend. From that day on, Charlene and I were more like sistas. We both shared each

other's secrets and each other's pain in the struggle to gain inner strength.

Chapter#6

Da Game

Journal Entry #40

Dear God,

I have a crush on this guy at school. I don't know his name but I sure do want to get to know him better. I'm not sure what kind of person he is in the inside but I do know that he is cute. I have heard great things about him from people who knew him quite well. I guess if it is meant to be, we will definitely meet.

Love,
Nia

Charlene and I went downstairs to the girls' locker room and changed into our cheerleading uniforms. The basketball game started at 7:00 p.m., and it was already 6:45 p.m. Coach Williams came into the locker room and blew her whistle.

"Now, girls, it is time for you to go upstairs to the gym, and I want you all to start warming up and practicing your cheers."

Charlene and I grabbed our blue and gold pom-poms and went up to the gym. Moments later, the crowd began to appear. The referee went to the middle of the gym floor with a microphone in his hand and began to announce all of the basketball players on both teams.

Tonight, Washington High School (Wild Cats) was playing Turner High School (Bulldogs). The referee called out the visiting team's names first. Turner's school colors were red and gold.

The spectators booed the visiting team. After the referee finished calling out the visiting team's names, he called out Washington High School's basketball players.

"Richard Allen, Bryan Clark..."

As the referee called out the names, the spectators applauded their home team.

The gym smelled like popcorn. Outside, there was a concession stand that sold pickles, popcorn, soda, hot dogs, nachos, candy, and other tasty items. I loved the popcorn because it was buttery and slightly salty, just the way I like it. Smelling the popcorn in the air made me very hungry.

"Maybe you'll see your mystery guy," said Charlene as we were sitting on the bleachers and observing what was going on.

"Gosh I hope so," I smiled.

"I'm going to go to the concession stand to buy some popcorn and a soda," I told Charlene.

"Me too, girl I was thinking the same thing."

Then I spotted him. On his jersey, read number 21.

Just then, Charlene poked me with her elbow. "Girl there he is!"

I stared hard at him and listening closely to what the referee was saying.

I watched as the mystery guy jogged to the middle of the gym and stood with his team mates; the players gave each other high fives and hit each other on the butt as they ran out to the middle of the gym.

The referee called out, "Clarence Walker."

So that's his name!

"Charlene, he's so cute!" I exclaimed.

"Calm down, girl," laughed Charlene.

"Man, he looks so good in his uniform."

The basketball game began. We went to the sidelines and started cheering.

The auditorium was filled with loud noise, as the spectators cheered for their teams. Turner High School was a prep school attended mostly by spoiled rich kids. Their cheerleading squad was very stiff and did mainly corny dorky-looking cheers.

Throughout the game, we cheered with lots of enthusiasm. Our team was winning the game. We cheered, "Get fired up, get fired up, get-fired-up-Hey!"

The cheerleading squad later yelled, "Washington Wild Cats are going to win, but Turner Bulldogs are going to lose!"

Clarence dribbled the ball and passed it to one of his team mates. Clarence ran down the court with his hands in the air as he waited for someone to pass him the ball.

He caught the ball in his hand and then dribbled. Once he got near the basket, he leaped in the air and executed a perfect slam dunk. I watched him glide though the wind in slow motion.

I cheered even louder and jumped up and down every time I saw him score.

The speaker called out, "And Clarence Walker made a slam dunk, that's another point for Washington High School...so far, Clarence has scored 18 points for his team and now the score is 42 to 12!"

The crowd roared, "Go, Wildcats, Go!"

Every time Clarence made a slam dunk, the spectators yelled, "Go, Clarence, Go!"

I looked at him in lust and bit my bottom lip. Gosh he is so fine. Clarence was sweating and his rippling muscles glistened. His muscular hairy legs were gorgeous; every time he jumped or ran down the court, the muscles in his arms and legs would tighten.

The cheerleading squad was so close to the basketball court, I had a chance to get a close look at him. I loved his intense brown eyes and lovely milk chocolate skin.

His hair was cut in a nice low hair cut filled with brushed waves. I wondered what it would be like just to run my fingers through his soft hair.

While cheering, Clarence walked right past me. Then he turned his head around to get a real good look at me. He smiled at me, and I smiled back at him.

After he smiled, he winked at me. I looked around to see if he was winking at someone else. When I saw no one else looking at him, I pointed to myself; he nodded his head 'yes' to imply that he was winking at me. I began to blush; I was so glad that Clarence had actually noticed me.

The game was over, and Washington High School had beat Turner High, 60 to 20.

Meanwhile, I found Charlene and told her what had happened. "...And Charlene, he noticed me!"

"Girl, that is so great, I'm so glad for you. At least Clarence noticed you quicker than Scott would ever notice me. Gosh, girl, you must be head over heels over this guy. I see you learned his name."

"Yeah," I added.

"Well, Nia, I'm going to walk out with Mary, I'll be waiting for you out front."

"OK!"

I went back inside the gym. I found my pom-poms by the bleachers.

Then, I saw Clarence dribbling the ball, still practicing even after the game; he was wearing his basketball jersey under sweat pants and sweat jacket.

Those muscular legs. He's so fine. I continued to admire his looks.

Clarence turned around and spotted me standing near the bleachers. I was about to leave.

He called out, "Hey! Hey! Hey! Wait up!"

I turned around.

"Yeah, you," replied Clarence as he jogged towards me.

He approaches me.

My hair, long and shiny, cascaded down past my shoulders, and my skin appeared to be almost flawless.

He gazed into my eyes and said, "I've been noticing you."

I looked up at him and smiled. "What do you mean, you been noticing me?"

"Exactly what I said," grinned Clarence.

"Really?" I asked, disbelief showing in my tone. I noticed how tall he was, I came up to his shoulders.

"Yeah, what's your name?" Clarence stared into my eyes.

I blushed and answered, "My name is Nia Chavez."

"Nia, that's a pretty name."

"Thank you." I looked away for a brief moment. I was still amazed that we were actually talking to each other.

"My name is Clarence, but most people call me Clay." He has to be at least six feet, three inches tall, I thought.

He was checking out my legs.

I looked up at him and admired how nice and tall and handsome he was.

"What grade are you in?" I asked.

"Oh, I'm in the twelfth grade."

"Oh, really?"

"Yeah. What grade are you in?" asked Clay.

"I'm in the eleventh grade."

"So you're a junior!" laughed Clay.

He had the prettiest white teeth that I have ever seen. *What a dream!*

"Maybe we can keep in contact with each other," said Clay, one eyebrow arched.

"Yeah, I would like that," I smiled.

I was embarrassed because I didn't have a phone; I was wondering whether or not to tell him about my phone situation. *Well, what the heck, if he really likes me, it won't matter whether or not I have a phone.*

"Um, um, um...I don't have a phone," I said softly, looking down.

"Don't worry about that; it's no problem. Here's my number," said Clay.

He wrote down his phone number on a piece of paper and gave it to me.

I was very impressed and surprised that it didn't bother him that I didn't have a phone, knowing this made me smile.

"Maybe we can go out sometimes? What are you doing after the game?" asked Clay.

"Well, Charlene and I were planning on going out for pizza. Do you want to join us?"

"Sure, the fellas and I was thinking about going out for pizza too. Maybe we could go together as a group," suggested Clay.

"Yeah that's a good idea," I agreed.

"OK, well I'm going to see if my friend Marcus wants to go."

"All right, we'll meet you all out front."

"OK we'll be out there in a few minutes," said Clay, turning around to go back downstairs to the boys' locker room.

I was looking good. I had on eye liner and lip gloss and it made me look a little bit older. My hair had lots of body and sheen; for the first time in a long time, I was having a good hair day. One side of my hair was pinned up in a comb, while the other side fell loosely on down past my shoulders.

After flirting with Clay, I went to the front of the gymnasium to meet Charlene. I spotted her sitting on a bench. I walked swiftly toward Charlene to fill her in on the latest news.

"Hi, Charlene," I said, trying to hold my excitement.

"Hey, girl, you just missed Mary. She left with Natasha, and they are going to get some pizza, too."

"Oh, really?"

"Yeah."

"Guess what!" I exclaimed.

"What?"

"I saw Clay right before I came out here and he asked if he and Marcus could join us."

"Really, is Marcus that cute light skin guy that Clay always hangs out with all the time?"

"Yeah, that's him."

"Great, then they can go with us and we can have pizza together."

Five minutes passed on by. Clay and Marcus finally came out front. Laughing and joking, we all headed to the Superb Pizza Restaurant on 21st Street. We had a wonderful time, and this was the beginning to a close friendship between Clarence and me.

Chapter #7

Photo Luv

Photography was my favorite class in high school. I loved learning about the proper techniques on how to capture present moments on film.

When I first registered for school, my guidance counselor told me that I could take an elective of my choice. I had a choice between drafting, graphic arts, and photography. I chose photography because I loved looking at the alluring photos of coffee house magazines.

Grandma Maria used to take me to coffee shops and I loved smelling the rich aroma of coffee in the air. Grandma used to love having her fresh coffee in the mornings.

Photography opened my eyes to the world of fashion and different cultures around the world. I loved looking at the brillant colorful photos of other countries and cultures in National Geographics. I enjoyed studing lively colors that jumps out through the camera lens. I often daydreamed of going to foreign places and taking pictures of new lands and learning more about other cultures.

Going to photography class everyday was my inspiration for going to school. Mrs. Miller was my photography teacher and was my favorite teacher in the whole wide world. I had a chance to learn about the history of photography. Mrs. Miller showed me several techniques to working with a camera. She inspired me to work for the school newspaper. Mrs. Miller loved my photos so much, that she enlarged my prints, then framed and hung it in the front hall of the school.

February 1986

After school, Mrs. Miller introduced me to the students who worked on the school newspaper. Most of the students on the school newspaper were upper classmen.

When I strolled in with Mrs. Miller, I spotted Clay sitting at a desk near an Apple computer. He was talking with other students about which articles were going to be published in the next news edition.

Clay looked up from the computer. Our eyes locked for a brief moment. Clay grinned and showed off his gorgeous teeth. I smiled back at him. He winked at me and I began to blush.

"Class, I found the perfect addition to the school newspaper and yearbook team. This is Nia Chavez and she will be the photographer. I will need for you all to coordinate with her on dates and times you all are going to do interviews and news stories so that she can take the pictures."

Mrs. Miller glanced at me.

"Nia I want you to get with Clay and Linda. They are in charge of editorials before they come to me," stated Mrs. Miller. I felt so good inside. I was excited that I was going to have chance to work on the school newspaper.

After Clay and Linda gave the assignments to the school editors and writers, Linda came over and introduced herself. Linda was a senior and an honor student. She was a mocha complexion and wore glasses.

Linda approached me.

"Hi Nia, I am Linda. I am pleased to meet you."

"Nice to meet you too."

Linda had a warm smile and friendly disposition. I knew that I was going to enjoy working with her.

Once Clay finished talking to some of the student writers, he approached me.

"What's up! I see we keep bumping into each other." He stared intesely into my face with a raised eyebrow.

"Yeah we are." I smiled.

He search my face with his piercing sexy brown eyes.

"Well come with me my princess and let's go for a walk," said Clay jokingly. He bowed as he pretended to be prince charming. He reached his hand out to me.

"Why thank you my prince." I giggled while playing along with him. I held his hand.

We left the classroom laughing in a warm embrace.

Chapter #8

Unfortunate Events

A week has passed by, and I did not hear from mama. I was hoping that mama had forgotten about the idea of me moving back home.

It was a Sunday, in February 1986. Charlene and I were getting ready for church. I pulled my hair up into a long pony tail and twisted it up into a thick ball. I had on a pretty light blue dress with small floral prints. Thelma bought me the dress last Christmas.

Charlene was hot curling her hair.

"Ouch!"

"What happened?" I asked.

"I just burnt my ear with the curling iron."

"I hate it when I do that. I have burnt myself plenty of times. Put some oil or cocoa butter on your ear," I suggested.

Charlene put some cocoa butter on her ear. "Wow, Nia it does feel much better!"

After getting dressed for church, Charlene and I went downstairs for breakfast.

Later, Thelma came downstairs. Thelma looked stunning. She was a healthy-sized woman with meat on her bones.

Thelma's face was round with deep dimples. She had on a sharp suit, it was beige colored with a nice hat to match.

"Gosh, Mrs. Thompson, you look real nice today," I complemented her.

“Why, thank you, dear!” Mrs. Thompson smiled at me as she searched through her purse for her keys.

“Charlene, do you have your Bible?” asked Mrs. Thompson.

“Yes, Mom, I have mines.”

“How about you, Nia?”

“Yes, I have mines, too.”

“Great, then we are ready to go. Come on, Joseph, let’s go.” Mrs. Thompson located her keys and we headed out the door. Joseph was so cute; he had on a navy blue suit with a red bow tie on the front of his white shirt. He was already snaggled tooth, and every time he smiled, he showed it off. This year Joseph had started the first grade and he thought he was real hot stuff especially since he knew how to read.

“Is Mr. Thompson going?”

“No, he has to work in the restaurant today,” answered Mrs. Thompson.

Mrs. Thompson drove us to Mount Zion Baptist Church. Mount Zion was a huge church that sat right on the edge of town. It was the biggest building on the entire block. The church’s temple could be seen from a distance.

Once inside, I could hear the choir singing. The choir wore red and white robes. The usher led us to our seats.

Mrs. Thompson began to clap her hands and stomp her feet to the beat. I stood up and I started clapping my hands. I loved listening to the uplifting sound of gospel music.

After the choir finished their selection, Pastor Peterson stood before the congregation. He was a short stocky man with dark chocolate skin. He had a bald spot on the top of his head that shined every time the light hits it. Charlene and I used to joke about rather Pastor Peterson’s glasses or head shined the most.

Once Pastor Peterson finished the altar prayer, he went right into his sermon. This Sunday, Mr. Peterson preached about faith and believing in God. I really focused on what he was saying; I found that hearing the words of God made me feel much better inside.

For some reason, I felt more at peace after praising the Lord. Grandma taught me how to pray. Every night Grandma and I used to get down on our knees and pray right before bedtime.

After church service, we went home and changed into some comfortable clothes while Thelma prepared collard greens, mashed potatoes, corn bread, and oven fried chicken.

Richard and Thelma were excellent cooks; people all over town loved to go to their Jamaican and soul food restaurant, *Thompson's Sizzling House of Food*. It was definitely the big talk all across town.

I went upstairs to work on my book report.

An hour passed by and when I completed my history report. I got up from the desk, feeling like I have accomplished something positive. A lot of times it was hard for me to just sit down and focus on doing my school work. Often times I lost interest in what I was doing.

I raced down stairs and headed straight to the kitchen.

"Hi, Mom," I said.

Thelma smiled.

"Hi, Nia, did you finish your report?"

"Yes, I did. Will you be able to read it later?"

"Sure, I'll do that after we finish eating dinner."

"Great! Is there something you need me to do?" I asked.

"Yes, you can make the salad and get the table set."

"OK, then."

I was about to leave, but, Thelma changed her mind and said, "Go tell Charlene I want her to set the table while you do the salad."

"OK."

After washing my hands, I went to the den and told Charlene, "Your mom wants you to set the table while I fix the salad."

"Aw, man! I don't feel like it!" complained Charlene.

I went back to the kitchen and I started washing the vegetables.

While I was fixing the salad, the phone rang. Thelma went to answer it.

"Hello."

On the other end of the phone was Rachael.

"Is my daughter there?" snapped Rachael.

"Yes, but she's busy now."

"Look, Nia is my daughter and I want to speak to her!"

"Look, Rachael! Haven't you hurt the girl enough?"

"Well, she is my daughter, and I want her to live with me!"

"I don't think that's a good idea."

"It doesn't matter what you think because, like it or not, she's going to be living with me and my new husband!" sneered Rachael.

"You just have to come into the picture and ruin everything don't you? Since she's been staying with us, her self esteem is so much higher and her grades have improved-."

"I don't have to listen to this bull shit!" Rachael rudely interrupted.

"Just tell her I want her to be here with her things by tonight!" yelled Rachael.

Click. Rachael hung up the phone.

"Well I be damned," uttered Thelma.

I knew that Thelma was talking to mama on the other line.

By Mrs. Thelma's facial expression, I knew that things were not good.

"Was that mama?"

"Yes, dear, that was your mother," answered Thelma sadly.

"What did she want?"

"She wants you to go back home with her tonight."

"What?" I asked in shock.

"Nia, she wants you to start packing up now and move back in with her by tonight," added Thelma.

"But I don't want to go back. She doesn't care about me!" I began to cry.

"I'm sorry Nia, but there's nothing I can do about it."

I fled up the stairs. Thelma called after me, but I just kept going.

I went into the bedroom. I plotted myself on to the bed and began to weep.

Mrs. Thompson knocked on the bedroom door.

"Come on in." I sat up sat up on the bed and wiped my teary eyes.

Mrs. Thompson walked in and sat on the other end of the bed.

"Nia, are you OK?" Mrs. Thompson placed her hand upon my shoulders.

"Yes, I'll be fine. It's just that all of this came to be a big shock, you know," my words trailed off as more tears formed in my troubled brown eyes. Mrs. Thompson got up and walked over to the night stand to get a box of Kleenex.

After handing me the box of tissue, she sat down next to me.

"About a week ago mama told me that she wanted me to move back in with her and Q I was hoping she would forget about the idea of me moving back in but she just had to call and ruin everything," I mumbled.

I felt very comfortable with Mrs. Thompson; I felt like I could really talk to her about almost anything. Mrs. Thompson listened as I poured my heart out to her. Thelma became teary eyes too.

"Nia, I know that all you are feeling right now is hurt, but you do have to go back to your mom because she does have custody over you."

I bit my bottom lip and nodded my head.

After our long discussion, we both went downstairs to join everyone for dinner. There was nothing but silence at the dinner table. Even little Joseph was quiet. Eating dinner that night was very strange; no one had anything to say. There was nothing but sadness in the air. I didn't eat much on my plate; I pretty much lost my appetite.

Once dinner was over, I went upstairs to pack. Charlene came into the bedroom to help me pack up the rest of my belongings.

"Nia, why don't you want my mom to know about your dark secret? If she knew that, she wouldn't let you go back to her," said Charlene while folding one of my sweaters to go inside my suitcase.

"I know, but I just don't want her to know. Charlene, you must keep this a secret, nobody should know about this. Please don't tell anyone," I pleaded.

Charlene looked worried.

"But Nia, I really do think that this is a serious matter and someone should know about what's going on."

"Charlene, I just don't want anyone to know about this. All of this is very embarrassing, and I don't want it to be known. Let's just forget about it. OK?" I insisted. I began forcing the rest of my clothing inside the suitcase.

We went downstairs with the suitcases and then outside to the car. Mrs. Thompson was already waiting in the car; she cranked it up and backed out of the drive way. The drive to my house was very quiet. The only sound that could be heard was the purring of the engine.

We reached James Monroe Housing.

All of us, walked in the cold dreary weather. It was two blocks to the dark rusty gates that led to James Monroe. Inside were some thugs and drug dealers hanging out, gulping down their forties, one of the men was Q

In the background, I could hear the sirens of police cars and ambulances driving through the war zones of the night.

We reached my building where I lived. As they went up the stairs, the steps made a loud squeaky noise. Mrs. Thompson turned up her nose when she saw all of the foul language written all over the walls and roaches crawling everywhere; we covered our noses when we smelled the awful pungent smell of urine.

We reached mama's apartment. I knocked on the door and moments later, Rachael answered the door. Mama stood in the doorway with a cigarette in one hand and her other hand placed on her narrow hip. She had pink hair rollers in her hair.

"Oh Nia, how's my Baby? I've missed you so much!" She gave me a hug.

"Hi, Rachael, we brought Nia over for you." Thelma was holding Joseph's hand.

"Ooh, hi." Rachael mumbled and rolled her eyes.

After grandma's death, mama asked Thelma to keep me because she knew that she was neglecting me. I almost burned down the apartment while being left home alone for the entire weekend. A social worker threatened to take me away from her if she didn't straighten up. Depressed and strung out on drugs Rachael begged Thelma to let me stay with her until she got her act together.

I could tell mama was some what agitated. Mama had bruises on her arms. Her eyes were puffy and her hair was a mess. She looked down at Mrs. Thompson's son.

"Is that your son?" Rachael asked. She had a stern look on her face.

Before Thelma could answer, Rachael released the smoke that she had inhaled from her cigarette and some of the smoke went into Thelma's face. Thelma frowned.

Rachael sneered when she saw Thelma's facial expression.

"Yes, this is my son and we're leaving because I see that we are not welcomed here."

"Ain't that's the truth." Rachael rolled her eyes.

I was very upset about the way mama was acting.

"Bye, Nia, I'll see you later," said Thelma. Charlene and Joseph waved good bye.

"Bye, Mrs. Thompson, I love you." I began to choke into tears.

"We love you too."

A moment later, I rushed after Mrs. Thompson and gave her a hug; I held on so tight that Mrs. Thompson had to tell me that I had to let go.

I began to weep.

"Come on, Nia, you need to come back inside. You're home with your real mama now," snapped Rachael.

I wiped my eyes and waved good-bye and went back inside.

Chapter #9

Silent Tears

Journal Entry #48

Dear God,
Every night he hurts me. I try so hard to be a good girl. Every night he has been violating me. I'm a virgin God and grandma taught me about the bible. Please God keep that monster away from mama and me. I am so scared and so confused. Please help me God.
Love,
Nia

The same night when I moved back home with mama, something very strange and peculiar happened. I was getting myself ready for bed that night. I pulled my long, thick, wavy brown hair into a bushy ponytail. After taking a shower, I put on my favorite purple and white unicorn pajamas. I got in bed and drifted off to sleep.

I was awakened when I felt like someone was watching me. I stirred and turned my head. I saw a figure standing in my doorway. I rubbed my eyes and then looked again; it was Q standing there. Seeing him standing there gave me the creeps. I sat up quickly and wrapped my blanket closer around myself. Q closed the door behind him and then approached me.

"What do you want?" I asked.

"Shhh," whispered Q with his index finger to his lips.

"Stay away from me!" I demanded.

"Shh," whispered Q once again.

He sat on my bed and placed his hand over my mouth. He started to violate me. With his other hand, he hastily unbuttoned my purple fleece pajama top and started caressing my breasts. I tried to push him away from me but he was too strong. He reached inside my pajamas and started to fondle me. He started fingering me roughly. Q was hurting me. I tried to scream but his hand was held firmly over her mouth.

After fondling me for twenty straight minutes, he let me go. I moved to the corner of my room and curled up in fear.

Q grinned and said, "See you later, sweet thang."

With that, he winked at me. I stayed in the same corner for the rest of the night and cried myself to sleep.

A week passed. Almost every night, Q came into my bedroom and took advantage of me. He threatened me and told me not to tell a soul.

One late afternoon, I decided to tell her mama what was going on. After school I went home. Mama was in the living room. Before saying a word, I checked the entire house to make sure Q was not home. He was not there.

As usual, mama was puffing on a cigarette and watching some talk show on TV. Mama was staring off into space; I could tell that she had just awakened from being high.

I gently tapped mama on the shoulder, "Mama, there's something I have to tell you."

Rachael stretched and yawned.

"Yeah what do you want, child?" asked Rachael.

"I want to tell you something about Q"

"What about him?"

"Mama, he's been, he has been feeling on me."

"You said what!"

"He's been touching me in places that are wrong," I added.

Mama slapped me across my face.

"How dare you make up such a damn lie? He's your stepfather. You're just jealous and don't want to see me happy!"

I rubbed my cheek. My face stung from the slap. I cried, because I knew in my heart that I was telling the truth.

"But Mama, I'm telling the truth," I pleaded.

"Go to your room and I don't want to see your face again, you no good heffa!"

I left the room and went to my bedroom. I was so hurt that mama didn't believe me, knowing this drilled a hole right through my heart.

The next Saturday night, Rachael and Q got into a fight.

I could hear the commotion from next door. I was over my friend's, Laporsha, house.

"Is that your mama fighting again?" asked Laporsha.

"Yeah, that's them. I'll be right back."

I went home. Through the door, I could hear Q yelling and cursing mama.

I unlocked the door. I was shocked at what I saw; Q was holding mama by the hair and was punching her in the stomach like a punching bag. Blood came out her nose and mouth. She had been beaten so severely that she was unconscious.

I leaped on Q's back and started punching him as hard as I could.

He grabbed me and threw me full force across the room. I hit the wall so hard that I was knocked out.

When I woke up, I saw a strange man with a little flashlight gazing into my eyes. I tried to get up, but my head started to spin.

"Don't try to get up so fast. You're suffering from a mild concussion."

"Where's my mama?" I asked.

"She's down the hall getting stitched up," answered the doctor.

"I'm Dr. Kawasaki. Here's an ice pack to put on the back of your head to relieve some of the pain and swelling."

"Where am I?" asked I as I rubbed my neck.

"You're at Soundview Health Center and you're all set," answered Dr. Kawasaki.

"Now you can go into the waiting room and wait on your mother," he added with a nice warm smile.

I slowly got up and went to the waiting room. My head started pounding. I placed the icepack back on my head. A few minutes later, a police officer approached me and asked me a few questions. His name tag read "Officer Hicks".

"Was your stepfather the one who beat up you and your mother?"

Officer Hicks was a medium built white man with brown hair and clear blue eyes. He appeared to be in his late twenties or early thirties. He looked very serious and was all about business.

"Yes, he did."

"We have arrested your step father."

After asking a few more questions for his police report, he left.

Later that night, mama and I were released from the hospital and we took a cab home. I was happy that Q was in jail because he could not hurt me no more.

The next morning, Q called and begged mama to get him out of jail. He promised that he would not hurt us again. Mama believed him. Q did his time in prison and was eventually released early for good behavior. Mom let Q come back home.

Right after Q got out of prison, he was still coming into my bedroom at night. I was tired of him hurting me. I desperately wanted for all of this to stop.

One day after school, I went to a hardware store and purchased a lock for my bedroom door. I set the lock so I could lock the door from inside, so no one could come in my room with out a key. I needed a lock not only to keep Q from molesting me, but to keep mama and Q out of the money that I was saving. They often stole my hard earned money, from working at the Thompson's restaurant, for drugs.

Night rolled around. After I got dressed for bed, I locked my bedroom and dozed off to sleep. I was awakened to the noise of Q at my door. He tried to open the door, but it was locked. He knocked on the door so hard it shook.

I jumped when he hit the door with so much force. I wrapped my blanket real tight.

"Nia, I know you're in there, so open up the fuckin' door and let your daddy in!"

I did not answer; I was too scared.

Q continued to pound on the door and tried to open it, but was unsuccessful. Tears were streaming down my cheeks; I feared that Q would do me a lot of harm.

Just when I thought he would get in, Q gave up.

"That's all right, don't open the fuckin' door!" He yelled furiously while kicking the door.

"Just remember that your ass is mines in the morning. You're gonna get a good old fashion ass whipping just like I gave you and your mother the other night!" Q roared.

I shivered. I wished that grandma was still alive or that I was still staying at Charlene's house; I felt so safe over there.

My bedroom window did not have a fire escape. So I decided that I was going to sneak into the bathroom in the morning and make sure Q was no where in sight when I left for school. And in the afternoon, I had no intentions of going back home. I would spend the night over the Thompson's house in an effort to avoid getting beat up by Q After analyzing what had took place and planning an escape route, I finally dosed off to sleep.

The sunlight beamed into my room. From outside, I could hear the sound of cars and people out on the streets. I yawned and stretched and rolled over to look at the clock to see what time it was; it was 7:15 A.M., and it was definitely time to get ready for school.

I got up and walked towards the door. Before going out of the door, I placed my ear against it to see if I could hear Q's presence. When I didn't hear or see anything after peaking out the door, I opened it wider and tiptoed out quickly and quietly to the bathroom. Before I could reach the bathroom, Q intercepted me with a dirty smirk on his face!

I looked up at Q in fear. My eyes were wide and my mouth sprung open in shock. The first thing I could think of was running. I turned around and started running. Q quickly caught me and yanked me by my pony tail. Then he started dragging my ruthlessly down the hall by my hair. I screamed in pain. Both of my hands went up to my head in an effort to try to keep him from pulling my hair out.

Once he dragged me to the kitchen, he started slapping me violently across my face. Eventually, his slaps turned into punches.

He punched me several times across the jaw and in the stomach. He grabbed my arm and yanked it hard; I heard my bones pop. Then he kicked me twice in the stomach and once in the back.

"Now I told you, bitch, that in the morning I was going to give you a good old fashion ass whipping for locking that door last night! Every time you lock the door, the more you are going to get beat down!" yelled Q He pointed his finger in my face.

Q rumbled through the drawer and pulled out a knife. He slashed my legs with it and stormed out of the house. I didn't move for a while because I was in so much pain. I couldn't move my left arm. All I could do was lay there and cry.

Slowly I lifted myself up and limped to the bathroom. I looked at myself in the mirror and my face looked horrible; he beaten me until I was literally black and blue.

I was very upset at the reflection I saw in the mirror. I was so upset that I banged my fist against the mirror in rage. My eyes were swollen, my lips were bloody and busted open, and my nose was bleeding. I could barely move. Whenever I tried to take in a deep breathe, I felt excruciating pain in my abdomen and lower back.

With a damp face cloth, I cleaned myself up. After cleaning the blood off my face and arm, I went back to the mirror to see if I looked any better; I still looked awful, and I knew that I couldn't possibly go to school looking like this.

I missed a day at school. I was at home all alone. My leg would not stop bleeding. I tried to wrap a clean cloth around my leg to slow down the bleeding but the blood would start to slowly seep through. I was beginning to feel very cold and weak.

There was a knock at the front door. At first, I didn't get up, but the second time I heard the knocking, I dragged myself out of bed to answer the door. I was feeling cold, dizzy and lightheaded.

Gosh, I wonder who that could be.

I looked through the peep hole to see who was there. I discovered that it was the Thompsons. I was so happy it was them.

I opened the door to let them in.

"Hi, Nia, how are you doing?" asked Mr. Thompson. My back was still turned to them; I was too ashamed to face them.

"Oh, I'm doing fine," I slurred.

"Well girl, aren't you going to come over here and give us a hug?" asked Charlene.

"Yeah," I answered.

I turned around and they saw my face.

They all looked at me in dismay.

"Oh my God, Nia what happened to your precious face?" asked Mrs. Thompson in shock.

Thelma gently cupped my face with both her hands, and tears filled both our eyes.

"Who did this to you?" asked Thelma.

"My stepfather."

"Mom, Nia needs to go to the hospital!" Charlene screamed.

Joseph started crying.

"Yes she does," agreed Mrs. Thompson through gritted teeth.

Mr. Thompson nostrils began to flare in anger. He folded his arms in front of him.

"Come on Nia, you're going with us."

I winced in pain as I tried to walk to my room to get my clothes. Reaching to help me, Mr. Thompson saw that I had a deep stab wound on my leg.

"Honey I'm going to take Nia to the car. She can't walk." Mr. Thompson grabbed a blanket and wrapped it around me. He then scooped me up in his arms and carried me to the car.

"It's going to be all right you are with us now. Little Champ." Tears filled my eyes.

The Thompsons rushed me to the hospital.

Chapter #10

Abuse

We reached Soundview Medical Center. After signing me in, we waited for a doctor to examine me. Two hours passed before a doctor saw me.

The doctor was an attractive, thirty-something, brown skinned woman.

"Sorry for the long wait, but we've had a lot of people rushed in here this morning."

She looked at my chart.

"So you're Nia? How did this happen?" Holding my chin, the doctor scrutinized my busted lips and swollen eyes.

"I got beat up," I slurred.

"Nia, I'm Dr. Young, and I'm going to take good care of you, OK?" smiled the doctor.

"OK."

"A nurse will be with you in a few minutes, and I'll be back shortly."

A nurse came and directed us to a room. Thelma pushed me in a wheel chair. It was a very cold room, so cold that it made me shiver. Thelma and the nurse helped me get settled on the hospital bed. Everything in the room was white.

"Here is a blanket sweetie." Thelma covered me with the blanket.

Half an hour later, Dr. Young came into my room; the nurse had already cleaned me up and examined my deep cuts and bruises. Sabrina, the nurse who took care of me, approached Dr. Young.

I could hear them discussing my situation.

"It looks like she's going to have to get some more stitches," said Sabrina.

"You mean to tell me you've seen this patient here before?" asked the doctor.

"Yes, I believe about a month ago both her and her mother were here to get treatment for their injuries. I think she had a minor concussion," answered Sabrina. She glanced back at me.

"We will be right back," said Dr. Young as they stepped out of the room to talk about me.

Dr. Young entered my room five minutes later.

"Hi, Nia, how are you doing?"

First the doctor examined my stiff arm.

"Nia, try to move your left arm."

I couldn't move it.

The doctor moved the arm slightly and I yelled "Ouch!" tears sprung to my eyes.

"Oh, dear, I'm afraid your arm may be broken." said Dr. Young.

"I'll need an x-ray of her arm," Dr. Young told the nurse assisting her.

The doctor sat down on a stool to take a closer look at my facial bruises and deep cuts. She also examined the bruises that covered my entire back.

The doctor gently pressed down on her back and asked, "Does that hurt?"

"Yes," I flinched as I felt a sudden surge of pain.

After examining me closely, Dr. Young took Mrs. Thompson aside and asked, "Are you her mother?"

"No, I'm her godmother. I watch after her whenever her mom is unable to or just don't feel like being bothered with her," answered Mrs. Thompson.

"Do you know where her mother is?"

"No, she's out in the streets somewhere."

"Do you know if there's any way to contact her?"

"No, they don't have a phone. I don't mean to be nosey, but Nia is very important to me. Why do you need to contact her mother? Is she going to be OK?" Thelma had a worried look on her face.

"She's going to be fine, Mrs. Thompson. You have nothing to worry about. But her arm is broken and she's going to need some stitches and some pain killers. Mrs. Thompson, do you know how long she's been in this condition?"

"Well, she told me that she was beaten up yesterday, and she has not been to a doctor because nobody has been home to take her until we came today. We discovered her in this condition."

"Do you know who did this to her?" Dr. Young took off her glasses.

"Yes, she told us that her stepfather did this to her."

"All right, then. She has to get some stitches and have a cast put on her arm. We can't wait to reach her mother so we're going to go right on ahead."

"OK."

Dr. Young had to first pop my bone back into place and put a cast on my arm; it was a painful experience for me but I took it very well.

Dr. Young quickly started working on the wounds.

Mrs. Thompson went to the waiting room while Dr. Young and the nurse stitched me up. After working on me for about an hour and thirty minutes, Dr. Young went into the waiting room and brought Mrs. Thompson back to my room. I was getting sleepy from the medicine that the nurses gave me.

"We're finished with Nia and right now she is resting," smiled Dr. Young.

"That's great. Did you have to put in a lot of stitches?" asked Mrs. Thompson. "All together we did fifty stitches. It appears that her stepfather may have used a sharp object to cut her this badly. She lost a lot of blood we are going to check her blood count. She might need a blood transfusion if she lost too much blood," responded the doctor.

Later, the police came and asked us some questions. I refused to talk because I was afraid Q would hurt mama. He told me that if I ever told anyone that he would kill both of us. I did not feel like talking to the police and they became quite pushy. Thelma tried to convince me to talk, but this only upset me even more. I began to break down into tears, so they left me alone.

"She has been traumatized over what had happened to her. She does not want to talk right now." Thelma put her arms around me and shook her head to the police with disapproval.

Two days later, I was released from the hospital, and Mr. and Mrs. Thompson took me to their house. After I got situated, Richard had to go back to the restaurant, but Thelma stayed to make sure I was OK.

I didn't go back to school for another week. Charlene brought my homework and class assignment home for me to do, so I wouldn't fall behind in school.

Throughout the week, many people came by to visit me. It really brightened my day when Coach Williams came to see how I was doing. The word was out at school that I was hurt and had to go to the hospital. Even some of the girls from the cheerleading squad came by to visit me.

I was really surprised when Clay came by to see me.

Mrs. Thompson went to Charlene's room and said, "There's someone here to see you, Nia."

I gradually got out of bed to put on my housecoat and went downstairs to see who was there to see me.

When I got around the corner, I saw Clay sitting on the couch looking as handsome as ever.

"Hi," I said softly.

"Hello," grinned Clay. He helped me sit down on the couch.

"Gosh, I'm so surprised to see you." I smiled.

"Yeah, I couldn't miss out on seeing my beautiful friend. I really miss you at school. I was wondering what happened to you."

"How did you know I was hurt?"

"Charlene told me." Clay looked at me. I had a huge bandage on my forehead and a cast on my left arm.

"Does it hurt?"

"Yes, a little bit," I glanced down at my arm and then looked at him.

"Word around school has it that you've been in a car wreck or got into a fight. There are so many rumors out about what happened to you that I don't know what to believe." Clay leaned back comfortably on the couch.

"Does it really matter how it happened?" I asked.

"No, but we're good friends. Why are you being so secretive about this whole thing?" Clay leaned over to take a good look at me.

I noticed Clay's gorgeous eyes were and wanted desperately to talk about something else.

"So, Clay how's your girlfriend?" I tried to change the subject.

"Who, you mean Sonya?" laughed Clay.

"Yeah, Sonya," I smiled.

"Well, we broke up."

"Really, what happened?" I was shocked to hear that, because Clay and Sonya had been dating each other for a long time.

"Both of us were getting tired of each other, so we decided to go our own separate ways."

Finding out that Clay had broken up with his girlfriend made me very happy. I knew this was selfish, but I always had a crush on Clay and wanted to be with him, but was too afraid to tell him.

Later that evening, Clay left. Talking to him had really made me feel better. I was happy that we have such a strong friendship. A lot of times, we walked home together because he also stayed in Castle Hill just like Charlene.

Social services were notified about my condition but no one was proactive enough in getting me out of my living situation. Thelma called social services on numerous occasions and the hospital documented the abuse but the social services system still continued to fail me.

Mama found out that Thelma reported her to social services. A social worker came by mama's apartment and was asking her a lot of questions about me; this made mama furious. So Rachael decided that she was going to try to get even with Thelma by calling the police on Thelma; she accused Richard and Thelma of trying to kidnap me. The police and the social workers from children services questioned and investigated the Thompsons and found out that Rachael was lying and so they let me continue to stay with the Thompsons.

Chapter 11

Sixteen

Journal Entry #56

Dear God,

I am enjoying my time with the Thompson's. I love the peaceful and loving home environment that surrounds me in their home; unlike the violent street environment that I always felt when I am with mama.

I still have nightmares of Q I just wished that it would all go away. God please continue to watch over me and keep me safe. Please show me the path to getting out of da hood.

Love,
Nia

I was happy when my cast was taken off, and I was still staying with the Thompsons. Rachael had started calling again and was raising hell about me living with them. After exchanging a few harsh words towards one another, the Thompsons reluctantly decided to let me go back home right after my birthday, on October 6th. They did not have much of a choice but to send me back to mama's house.

Mrs. Thompson knew that my birthday was coming up so she wanted to do something special for me. On Friday, the day after my sixteenth birthday, the whole Thompson family got together and threw me a surprise birthday party. Right after Charlene and I came back from the mall that evening, I got the surprise of my life.

As Charlene and I walked toward the Thompson's apartment building, we noticed that the lights were off in the living room from the street and no cars were parked outside.

"Gosh, that's strange, nobody's home," I observed.

"Yeah, I guess they had to go somewhere." said Charlene as we walked up the steps.

Charlene reached down inside her purse and pulled out the keys to unlock the door. The door made a squeaky noise as she opened it.

"It's dark in here. Let me turn on the light."

Once I turned on the light, I heard voices of other people in the room.

"Surprise!" yelled everyone who was hiding behind the corner.

I turned around and saw all of my friends, all the people I loved and cared about.

I was more than surprised, I was flabbergasted.

"Happy birthday, Nia!" smiled Thelma, giving me a big warm hug.

I was so happy that I became teary eyed. I hadn't had a birthday party since Grandma Maria gave me one when I was nine years old.

Gradually, I looked around at the small crowd to see who were there. I saw Mary and Laporsha. To my right, I spotted Clay and Marcus standing near the table with the food; as usual, the two of them were ready to dig into the food.

"We got you, didn't we?" laughed Charlene.

"Yeah, you all really surprised me with this one," I smiled.

"Nia, come on over here and blow out the candles on your cake." Thelma gestured for me to come over.

Mrs. Thompson knew exactly what kind of cake I liked: strawberry short cake. On top of the cake, it read, "Happy Birthday Nia." I looked down and counted the sixteen candles.

"Make sure you make yourself a wish!" sang Mrs. Thompson.

I made my wish; I closed my eyes and wished for a bright future. After making my special wish, I opened my eyes and blew out all the candles. Everyone cheered and clapped. Then, we dug in and ate plenty of food. On the table, there were Buffalo wings specially prepared by Mr. Thompson with his secret sauce. There was also pizza, finger sandwiches, potato chips, dips, vegetables, cake, and punch. The aroma of the rich foods made everyone hungry. I had a chance to open my present from Richard and Thelma. They both bought me the camera that I always wanted. I was so thrilled. Now I could go and take all the photos I wanted. Tons of thoughts flooded my mind as I thought about the many images that I could capture with the camera. I was so excited. I ran over and hug both Richard and Thelma. Tears sprung to my eyes.

"Thank you."

"You are welcome."

In the background, music was playing on the entertainment center. All of my friends had brought cassette tapes over. Most of them loved listening to Michael Jackson's Thriller album, some Run D.M.C, and some jams from Atlantic Starr.

After eating, everyone went into the den, to dance. Clay, Marcus, Brandon, and Ramón competed with each other, showing off their break dancing moves; everyone stood around and watched them dance. After that, everyone started dancing themselves and we were having a real good time.

Someone turned on some slow jams. I was, helping Mrs. Thompson wash some of the dishes in the kitchen. Clay peeked in.

"Can I dance with the birthday girl?"

"Umm," I mumbled.

"Girl, go dance and have some fun! This is your party. I can handle cleaning up," laughed Thelma with her hands on her hips.

Without saying a word, Clay took me by the hand and led me to the den. It was very dim in there. Once we got to the middle of the floor, we started slow dragging. I looked around and spotted Charlene dancing with a guy name Robert. Clay placed his arms around my waist and I put my arms around his neck. The song was "Sexual Healing" by Marvin Gaye.

He whispered in my ear, "You smell so good." Hearing this made me blush. Clay gently ran his fingers though my long soft hair. I looked up and smiled at him, and he smiled back.

I wore some tight Jordache jeans, a purple sweater, and white Reeboks tennis shoes. Clay's hands moved down to my butt and he gently grabbed it. I felt uncomfortable, so I moved his hands back to my waist.

Clay leaned over and gently kissed me on the cheeks. He then kissed me on the lips. The kiss was very passionate, sweet, and gentle. I started to feel strange vibes that I have never felt before, and I kissed him back. Our intimate moment was broken when a rap song blared through the speakers.

Clay searched my face with his intense eyes and took me by the hand to lead me outside. We went to the roof of the building and sat down on the steps to talk. The sky was very clear, and the moon and stars shined ever so brightly in the sky. It was about 30 degrees, so I put on my coat to keep warm.

"Nia, there's something I want to tell you," said Clay, turning to look at me. He reached over and took my hand, looking deeply into my eyes.

"What do you have to tell me?" I smiled softly, playing with the draw string to his Starters jacket.

"Well, it's not exactly what I have to tell you, but what I want to ask you. Will you be my girlfriend?" Clay's voice was nervous and shy.

"I thought you'd never asked," I smiled. "Of course, I will!"

"Really?" asked Clay unbelieving.

"Yes," I inclined.

"Great!" yelled Clay as he stood up.

Clay reached over and helped me to stand up.

"You just don't know how much this means to me. Nia, since the first time I laid eyes on you, I always wanted you to be mines," he held my hands firmly in his. Clay pulled me closer to him and hugged me. He kissed me gently on the lips which gradually lead to a delightful French kiss.

Right after midnight, Clay and I went back inside. Almost everyone was getting ready to leave, except for some of my girlfriends who were staying for the slumber party. We stayed up all night, listening to *New Edition* records, watching horror movies, stuffing ourselves with popcorn and soda, and talking about various things, mainly boys. The next morning everyone was tired and bleary eyed.

After the girls left, Charlene and I cleaned up the house.

October 1986

A week after my sixteenth birthday, I had no other choice but to return back home. I really dreaded going back and I hated being there when I knew that Q was still around. There was a warrant for Q's arrest but he has not been caught by police. I was really scared because I did not know what to expect when I came home. My stomach was really turning because I had a bad feeling about going back. I was so afraid of Q I did not know what else he was going to do to me. I did not have any other place that I could go to. I felt so vulnerable and so alone. *God please take me out of this place called home.*

When Mrs. Thompson dropped me off to my mom's house, no one was there. I went to my bedroom to start unpacking. I heard the front door open and then close. It was Q He was coming down the hallway towards me. His face was filled with anger. He began to approach me.

"I see that you finally made it back home."

"Yeah, where is my mama?"

"Your mama is out turning tricks and she is not here to try to save your ass." He grinned and gave an insinuating look. My heart started beating fast and my eyes became watery. I knew that he was going rape me.

"Please don't." I shook my head no.

"No baby doll you are all mines tonight. I've wanted this for a very long time." Q closed and locked the door behind him. He began licking his lips in lust and grabbed his crouch.

I ran to the other side of the room. There was no other place to run. I tried to run past Q. Q quickly grabbed me. I tried to break free from his forceful grip. He picked me up.

"Put me down!" I yelled from the top of my lungs. He threw me down on top of my bed. He pinned me down and began slapping across my face. Each hit stung and hurt and knocked the wind out of me. I tried to push him off but he was too strong. He over powered me.

"Shut up bitch!"

He was hurting me as he pushed me down with his large hands.

Q ripped my blouse open and tore off my bra. My breasts were exposed. He stared at my breast in lust and began grabbing them with his rough hands.

All I could see was rage and anger in eyes. His eyes were like pools of darkness. He literally looked like the devil to me. He started sucking and biting on my tits.

He yanked my pants off of me and tore off my panties. I could smell the fowl smell of alcohol under his breath. I tried to turn my head away. He forced me to kiss to him. He continued to kiss me roughly. He stuck his filthy tongue inside my mouth.

Q unzipped his jeans and forced himself inside of me. He roughly covered my mouth to prevent me from screaming. It hurts so bad I felt like I was being ripped apart. Tears continued to roll down my cheeks. I felt like a piece of me was being taken. I did not want to believe that this was actually happening to me. It seemed like he was getting a thrill out of hurting me. I tried to pretend that I was some place else and this was not happening to me.

"Damn your stuff is so nice and tight. I am gonna have to rip it apart!" He thrust himself harder and harder. The deeper he went the more pain I felt. I winced in pain as he continued to rape me.

Q's sweaty body was all over me. He disgusted me so much that I wanted to throw up. I felt so used and violated. He finally came and got off of me. He got up and zipped up his pants.

"Baby Doll you have some good pussy. You might as well get used to it because I will continue to take some of your sweetness. Who knows, maybe I can sale it to the highest bidder!"

When he left, I snuck out. I did not know if Q was coming back but I was not about to wait and find out. I was so hurt and upset. It was a very stormy night I wanted to go to Charlene's house but it was further out. I knew that Clay's house was closer. I ran as fast as I could to get to his house. I climbed up the fire escape until to where his bedroom was. I tapped on the window seal. It was raining hard and I was cold from the rain. Fortunately Clay was in his room. He looked out of the window and saw that it was me. He opened his window. It started thundering and lighting.

"What are you doing here? It's late it almost midnight," he whispered.

"Clay, can I stay with you tonight. I'm scared." I was crying and shivering from the cold.

"Sure." Clay helped pulled me into his room.

"What's wrong, Nia?" I broke down into tears.

Clay reached over and hugged me. He kissed me on the forehead.

He closed and locked the door to his room. I was soaked from the rain.

"Please hold me, Clay. I so tired of him hurting me."

Clay took of my wet jacket and wrapped me up in a warm thick blanket.

He shared his bed with me. I snuggle up in the protection of his warm arms and drift off to sleep. Every since that night I went over to Clay's house to spend the night.

November 1986

Every since Clay and I started dating, we would always meet up for lunch along with some of our friends.

"Nia I would like for you to come to my house after school on Friday to meet my grandma and also my bother and sister. Can you come on Friday?"

"Sure."

"We can meet up after school but I would have to stop by the Boys & Girls Club to pick up my bother and sister. I hope you don't mind."

"Nah, that won't be a problem. I look forward to meeting them."

"Cool."

I smiled and Clay grinned back. He reached over and held my hand.

Friday rolled around and Clay and I met up after school. I had to go to cheerleading practice and Clay had basketball practice. We both met after our after school activities. I was carrying a heavy book bag. Clay reached over and carried my book bag for me. *What a gentleman.* I looked at him in a daze.

"Thank you."

"You are welcome." He grinned.

We both headed to the Boys and Girls Club to pick up Clay's brother and sister (Calvin and Ciara).

"So, Clay, where is you mom and dad? You don't talk about them very much?"

"Oh, it's a long story." Clay signed.

"We have a little time, don't we?"

"Well I guess. To make it short, my mom is in jail and my father is dead." He glanced at me.

"Oh, I am so sorry to hear that Clay."

Sadness was written all over his face. I reached over to caress his arms and gently squeezed his hands for reassurance.

"It's Ok; it has been two years ago. I'll talk to you about it later."

"Ok."

We reached the Boys and Girls Club.

Clay's brother, Calvin was ten and his sister Ciara was five yeas old. When I saw them, I could see the strong resemblance between them especially in the eyes. Ciara was a cute little girl. She was mocha complexion with wavy hair. Her hair was combed into pig tails. Calvin was a milk chocolate complexion with a neat low hair cut.

"Clay is this Nia, your girlfriend?"

"Yes she is." Clay looked at me with a raised eyebrow.

"She is beautiful." Calvin smiled and stared at me.

"No little Bro, you can't have her because she is mines." Clay puts his arms around my shoulders.

"She is pretty just like you said she was," said Ciara.

"Why thank you. "I started to blush.

"Clay I am hungry can we go by the candy lady's house?" Ciara pointed her small index finger.

"No, Ciara, we have to eat dinner. Grandma will be mad if you eat candy before dinner."

"Ah, Man!" Ciara poked out her lips.

We reached his grandma's house. They lived right off of Jefferson Place. Clay opened the door to their home. As we strolled in I could smell the rich aroma of southern style cooking.

Clay's grandma was in the kitchen cooking.

The house was very warm and cozy. I notice the flowered patterned sofa in the living that was cover in plastic. There were family pictures that were hung along the walls and along the stair case. One picture stood out the most to me and that was the picture of Clay's grandma and granddad. They were both posing together in black and white photo from the 1940's. His grandfather was wearing his military uniform.

"Grandma we're home."

“I’m in the kitchen.” We could hear pots and pans rattling in the kitchen.

Calvin and Ciara ran to the den and started watching TV.

Clay went into the kitchen to see about his grandma.

“I followed Clay to the kitchen. His grandmother was in her wheel chair. She leaned over the oven to try to get to the corn bread out of the oven.

“Grandma you need to rest. I will get the cornbread out of the oven. She moved out of the way to let Clay get the cornbread out.

I noticed that Clay’s grandma only had one leg. The other leg was amputated.

“Grandma did you take your medicine?” Clay washed his hands and started washing dishes.

“Yes, I did.”

Mrs. Moore had silver colored hair and was chestnut complexion.

“Grandma, Nia is here.”

“Hi, Mrs. Moore.” Mrs. Moore smiled.

“Oh hi dear, how are you?” I have heard so much about you from Clay.”

“Clay, tell your bother and sister to set the table and that dinner is ready.”

“Ok, Grandma.”

Mrs. Moore approached me in her wheel chair.

“So you are Nia.” Mrs. Moore was very sweet but also very stern.

“Yes, I am.”

“What a pretty, young lady you are. Clay has told me so much about you.”

Thank you, Mrs. Moore.” I smiled.

“How old are you?” Mrs. Moore was drying the dishes.

“Oh I’m sixteen.” Mrs. Moore glanced at me.

“Oh you are quite young.” she added.

Mrs. Moore spread some butter on top of the warm cornbread. I was quite amazed at how well Mrs. Moore was adapting to her new wheelchair. She dropped the spoon on the floor.

She was trying to bend over to pick it up.

“I’ll get it for you.”

“Oh bless you, child.”

The kids set the dinner table and everyone had dinner.

After dinner, Clay and I left.

Clay took me by my hands.

"Where are we going?"

"We're going to a secret place where we can be alone."

"You'll see. So Nia, what did you think of my grandma?"

"I like her she is so sweet."

"Yes, she is."

"Clay, where are you taking me? Why aren't we going to the park?"

"We are not going to the park. I am taking you to the basement."

Clay took me behind their building and we went down a set of steps. He unlocked the door and inside was a small apartment.

"Wow, Clay this is cool!"

"Yes it is, grandma was thinking about renting it out but changed her mind."

We both took off our coats.

"Are you cold?"

"Yes."

"I'll turn on the heater." Clay adjusted the thermostat.

"Clay this is so neat."

"Yeah, I usually come down here to hang out with the fellas."

"Wow!"

"This can be your haven, Nia."

"What?"

"Nia, I want you to stay here."

"Clay I don't know about that."

I looked around and it looked so cozy. There was a small T.V. on the dresser. There was couch that folded into a bed. There was a bathroom also.

I sat down on the sofa.

"Who did this to you?" Clay noticed the bruises on my arms. I saw the concerned expression written all over his face.

"Oh it is nothing." I put my jacket back on.

Clay came over and pulled up the sleeve to my jacket and examined the bruises that were all over my arm.

Clay gritted his teeth in anger.

"Who did this to you, Nia?"

"Clay, don't worry about me. I will be fine." I rubbed my arm.

"No it is not. Every time I see you have a bruise on your arm or a cut on your forehead. And you were out of school for at least 2 weeks and no one knows what happened to you. Two weeks ago you ran to my house in the middle of the night crying. What's going on Nia?"

"It's nothing Clay. Let's get off the subject."

"You are my girlfriend and if someone is hurting you I need to know about it. How can I protect you, if you don't tell me who he is?"

I bit my lip and looked away. I wanted to tell him but I worried about Clay's safety. I knew that Q was a very dangerous criminal and gangster drug lord in the South Bronx. He has already threatened to kill mama if I told a soul. I did not want to see any one else getting hurt. Q already threatened to make Mr. Thompson go out of business.

I looked at him and I knew that he was not going to let it go.

I got up from the couch and went to the window and looked out at the drizzling snow.

"Clay can you keep a secret?"

"Yes, I can."

"Clay, it's my stepfather Q He is a very dangerous man and his gang is heavily into drugs and prostitution. He told me that if I told a soul that he was going to kill my mother." I rubbed my arm. My eyes became watery.

"Gosh, I'm sorry Nia." He reached over to hug me in a strong embrace.

"Ouch!" I flinched as I felt a sudden surge of pain.

"Clay lifted up my shirt and saw bruises along my back."

Clay balled up his fist and his nostrils flared.

"Did Q do this too?"

I nodded my head and tears filled my eyes. I was so ashamed. Clay now knew a part of my dark secret. But he still did not know about the rape.

Clay pounded his fist against the wall, in anger.

I turned around and hugged Clay. He placed his arms around my slender waist. I laid my head against his strong solid chest; I could hear his heart beating. I signed because right then and there I knew that I was safe and secure.

Chapter 12

Richard Meets Thelma

The trees were bare from the Arctic Blast that past through Bronx, New York. The snow was drizzling outside and landed amongst the brown stone buildings and city streets. The snow brightened the urban view and amplified the feeling of Christmas.

I was really looking forward to the Christmas dinner at the Thompsons. The Thompsons invited all of their relatives over for Christmas dinner.

Mr. Thompson had seven brothers and sisters. I loved hearing the amazing stories that he would share about how he came to America and how he met Thelma.

The Christmas dinner was supposed to start at 2:00 P.M. Mr. Thompson was in the kitchen getting the dinner really. He was wearing his favorite blue apron.

I went into the kitchen to see if he needed any help.

"Mr. Thompson do you need any help?"

Richard was moving hastily in the kitchen."

"Yes, I do. Don't tell Thelma that I let you help me. I had to kick that woman out of the kitchen because she is too damn bossy!" Richard shook his head and wiped down the counter to add the garnishments to his turkey.

Richard was a dark chocolate complexion and bald headed. He was losing his hair so he had recently decided to go ahead and shave off all of his hair and go bald. I personally thought that he looked better. The bald look fitted him very well. He was short stocky man and was clean shaven with a neatly trimmed mustache and goatee.

"But I love that Thelma; I guess that is why I am still married to her. You are my partner in crime, Champ." He winked at me.

Richard spoke so fast that I had to absorb what he was saying. I could see where Charlene got her fast talking ways from. I started laughing to myself as I thought about how fast they both talk.

"Here champ put on your apron and start putting my special sauce over the chicken." I never did quite understand why Mr. Thompson called me Champ. But I am going to ask him one day why he made champ my nickname.

Everyone started to arrive around 3:00 p.m. instead of 2:00 p.m.

"Mr. Thompson, why is everyone arriving late? I thought dinner was supposed to have started at 2:00 p.m."

"Well, Champ, we are on black folk's time. Our relatives never come on time to these things." Richard chuckled.

Richard looked at his watch and clapped his hands.

"Ok, now I need for you to start putting the chicken into the serving dish."

"Ok, Mr. Thompson."

I helped Mr. Thompson set up the dinning room table. We set the kitchen up buffet style.

"Thanks Champ, I couldn't have done it with out you." Mr. Thompson smiled.

"You are welcome." I smiled back.

Once everyone arrived, the family mingled with one another and placed their gifts under the Christmas tree.

Richard gathered the family to the kitchen to get their dinner.

"Wow, Baby, you did a wonderful job." Thelma hugged Richard and they kissed each other on the lips.

"Thanks Honey. But I could not have done it with out my little champ over here. Mr. Thompson reached over and gave me a hug.

Everyone sat down to eat. I enjoyed every moment. Four hours later the dinner came to an end.

The dinner went over like a bang. Charlene and I helped with getting the house back in order. Charlene started telling me about how her mom and dad met.

"Nia you should really hear the story about how my dad came to America and how mama and daddy met."

"Wow, I would love to hear it."

"Yeah, I would tell you the whole story but I believe that my dad gives a better account as to what happened."

"Let me see if I can get him to tell the story." Charlene put the broom back into the closet.

"Daddy!" Charlene called Richard from the staircase.

"Yes, what is it?" Richard came down the stairs.

"Daddy, Nia never heard the story about how you came to America and how you and mama met."

"Sure, I would love to share my story with those who are willing to listen."

"Well Little Champ, let me share my story with you guys." Richard went to the bookshelf and pulled out a large brown leather photo album with gold trimming.

"You know I love sharing my stories with pictures because pictures tell a thousand words."

Richard sat down between Charlene and me on the sofa in the den. Across from us on the other side of the room was the lit fire place and the coffee table was right in front of us. The Thompson house was traditional in style. There was a large painting on the wall that looked like the same painting from the 70's T.V. sitcom "Good Times."

Mr. Thompson put on his reading glasses.

"Ok girls, everything for me begins when I was born in a Kingston, Jamaica in 1943. I was the fifth child of seven brothers and sisters."

Richard showed us black and white photos of seven little children. They ware dressed in 1940's attire. The girls had dresses and the boys had on knickerbockers pants with suspenders. All of them were barefooted. Richard sat there for a moment as he studied his childhood photos.

"I have so many good memories growing up in Jamaica." Richard shook his head and smiled. I loved hearing Mr. Thompson strong Jamaican accent.

"My family used to work in banana and sugarcane fields during the late 1940's. I was just a little boy." Richard pointed to the black and white photo of his family working out in the fields.

"My brother, Ralph, moved to the United States in 1960 and he told me that there were great opportunities here. Right after I finished school I saved up my money so I could I moved to America. I had to work hard out in the fields to make money especially since there was not much opportunity in Kingston. Once I saved up enough money, I migrated to the U.S. in 1964. I was very fortunate to find decent job working at a factory as a welder in Queens, New York." Richard showed a picture of him with his welding hat and equipment inside of the old factory building.

"Dad, tell Nia about how you and mom met." Charlene smiled.

"Sure Sweetheart."

Richard thumbed through the photo album until he found the photos during the time period in which he first met Charlene's mom.

"Oh here it is. This is the picture of the apartment building where I first met your mom in 1967."

"Was it love at first sight?"

"Oh no, it was far from that. I am afraid that Thelma did not care for me too much." Richard shook his head no.

"What?" I looked at him is dismay. I was very surprised because it seemed like Mr. and Mrs. Thompson was a happy couple.

"As a matter of fact I couldn't stand him." Thelma overhead their conversation from the kitchen.

"Oh Honey, I wasn't that bad was I?" Richard laughed.

"Oh yes he was it. I thought of him as a selfish short little man." Thelma stood by the door way with her hands on her hips.

"But good things do come in little packages, don't they dear?" Richard winked at Thelma.

"Yes they do dear and that is why you will always be my hero." Thelma smiled and waved off into the kitchen.

"Well any way I met Thelma at the apartment complex that I used to stay in Queens. When I first laid eyes on her I knew that she was the one for me. But your mama on the other hand was not least bit interested in me."

"Who was mom interested in then?" asked, Charlene.

"She like this thug, whatchacallit.um," Richard was trying to remember his name. He began to scratch his bald head.

"Honey! What is that no good thug you liked when we first met!"

Thelma came back into the den.

"Oh his name was Marco."

"Marco! What kind of name was that?" Charlene had crossed look on her face.

"Here he is. That's Marco." Richard pointed to Marco's picture in the photo album. I studied the picture for a moment. Marco was a sandy brown complexion. His hair was processed and had long side burns. He had on a black letter jacket and was holding a cigarette in his hand. I noticed the mischievous look in his eyes.

"Your mom was dating Marco at the time and would not give me the time of day. She always told me that I was too short for her and that I was not her type. But all of that changed during the summer of 1968."

"What happened in 1968?" Charlene and I said it at the same time. We both laughed at what just took place.

"Well I saved your mother's life. The apartment complex caught on fire. Everyone was trying to escape from the fire. Marco pushed your mother out the way to try to get out and she fell and hit her head. Marco did not bother to try to help her. The fire fighters noticed that everyone has escaped the flames but I noticed that Thelma was no where to be seen."

"That's terrible!" I could not believe that someone could be so cold. But then again, I knew that Q was like that. So that did not surprise me that a ruthless street thug would do such a thing.

"The firemen would not go back in so I took it upon myself to go get Thelma. I dodged some of the flames. I saw Thelma lying on the staircase. So I picked her up and I carried her to safety within a nick of time. Right after I got my Baby out of the building, the Building collapsed. It was like God gave me enough time to get Thelma out of there."

"Wow Dad, that's so amazing."

"Here is the newspaper clipping." Richard pointed to the news clipping and it shows him carrying Thelma out of the burning building.

I sat there and studied the photo in the news clipping.

"And that is why I call your dad, my hero because he saved my life." Thelma came into the den and smiled at Richard. Love and admiration for this man was written all over her face.

Richard got up and hugged Thelma. They both kissed.

"And we have been together since." Richard and Thelma stared intensely into each other's eyes.

Later that evening I thought about Mr. Thompson's story. Hearing his story really touched me. I always wanted a father figure in my life. From that day forward he became the fatherly figured that I yearned to have in my life. I looked at every photo in their album. Even though the Thompson's were not my family, they were the example of the type of family that I would like to have when I grow up.

That night I said a prayer to god. *"God if you can hear me. I have one wish. Please let me have a family like the Thompson's one day. Thank you, God. In Jesus name, Amen."*

Chapter 13

Q's Threats

January 1987

Often times Mr. Thompson would take Charlene and I to his restaurant. He especially needed us at the restaurant when he was short staffed, or has an influx of customers, or when ever he was catering an event. Sometime the whole family would work in the restaurant until the crowd died down.

Richard's business was really booming and this often times kept him so busy. I usually helped Mr. Thompson with cooking, Charlene greeted the customer's and took their orders and assist with busing tables, and Thelma was responsible for the book keeping. I was a good cook and I would assist Mr. Thompson with cooking and preparing food. Charlene was quite the chatter box and was great at greeting and mingling with customers. The customers literary adored her. Even little Joseph was put to work with washing tables and sweeping the floors. Thelma was very organized and was real good with numbers and accounting. Saturday and Sundays were the restaurant's busiest days.

One Saturday evening, I was in the kitchen helping Mr. Thompson with preparing his Jerk chicken and curry chicken dishes. The restaurant was closed but we were still working to prepare meals for a wedding on the other side of town. Working with Richard brought back memories of how I used to help my grandma with preparing Sunday dinner, I adored grandma's chicken, which was flavored with various spices and seasoning. *Arroz con pollo* (chicken with rice) was grandma's best chicken dish from Puerto Rico. I remember her telling me how arroz con pollo was brought long ago to the U.S mainland. Grandma's other prized chicken dishes included variation in chicken in sherry (*pollo al jerez*), *pollo agridulce* (sweet and sour chicken), and *pollitos asados a la parrilla* (broiled chickens). I still have a copy of grandma's special handwritten recipes in a book that she gave to me right before she died.

I loved working in the kitchen. I learned a lot about Jamaican cuisine from Mr. Thompson and soul food from Mrs. Thompson. The couple requested both Jamaican and soul food as their menu items for their wedding. All the food was already prepared. Richard and I began to pack the food. Charlene and was up in the front with the other staff washing down tables and putting the chairs away.

"Ok Nia now read me out the selected menu items off the list so that I can make sure we have packed everything correctly for the wedding."

I read everything to him on the list and everything was there. When we finished packing the food, there was a sudden loud noise in the front of the restaurant. Charlene and Joseph came to the back of the restaurant. Thelma came into the kitchen too because she heard the noise too.

"What was that?" Thelma had a worried look on her face.

"They looked like some street thugs standing in front of the restaurant. I told them that we were closed but they refused to leave. They insist that they wanted Nia."

Everyone looked at me. My heart started pounding because I knew who it was. It was Q and his street gang. They have been pushing Rachel to try to get me to move back home.

"It may be Q, my stepfather." My eyes became watery.

I peeked around the corner out the window and sure enough it was Q and his street gang. I bit my lip and leaned my head against the wall. I was so scared because I did not want to go back home. I knew that living environment at mama's house was not a good situation for me. My emotions were written all over my face.

"It is him isn't it?" Richard placed his hand upon my shoulder.

I nodded, yes.

Q's gang started hitting the glass to the restaurant. The shattering of glass could be heard to the back of the restaurant.

"I know that you all are back there!" yelled Q

Mr. Thompson went to the back of the restaurant to get his gun.

"Richard what are you doing?" Thelma had a worried look on her face.

"I am about to kick some asses! No one come by and threatened my family! Thelma, go call 911 and keep the children back here for safety."

"Ok dear. I love you." Richard and Thelma kissed each other on the lips.

Thelma took us back into the office and locked the doors. Thelma called 911.

I could hear Richard and Q yelling at other and exchanging words with one another. Then I suddenly heard a gun shot. I started screaming and hollering. About five minutes later we heard sirens at the front of the restaurant.

About twenty minutes later, it seemed like an eternity we heard a sudden knock at the door.

Thelma did not open the door. Keys started rattling against the door and the knob to the door turned. My heart was beating very fast and my palms were clammy. Richard was at the door. I let out a sign of relief.

"They are gone they fled when they saw the police coming." Mr. Thompson fist was bleeding and he had a busted lip.

I was so thankful that he was still alive. We all hugged each other in this moment of tragedy.

Chapter 14

Hurt

January 1987

I began to feel like I was a burden to the Thompsons. I overheard Mr. and Mrs. Thompson arguing about me. I knocked on their door one evening, but there was no answer. I cracked open the door and peeked in.

"Nia is not our daughter and not our responsibility! We should stay out of their family affairs, and let them work it out themselves!" argued Mr. Thompson.

"But honey, I love Nia like she's our own-."

"But she's not our own, don't you see that?" interrupted Mr. Thompson.

"Richard I know that you love Nia like your own. Why are you talking this way?"

"Thelma, I was threatened by Q's street gang again. They came by the restaurant and threatened me by gun point! He said that if we did not bring Nia back that I was going to pay."

"Did you call the police?"

"Yes and the police told me that there is nothing that they can do about Nia because we do not have custody over her."

"I know Honey, but Nia can't go back to that environment, it just is not good for her."

"I know, Baby. But we can barely pay our bills with two children. And now we have another mouth to feed. We just can't afford having her here."

I could not bare to hear anymore, so I left. I went to Clay and my secret spot the roof top over looking the city. The roof top was Clay and I thinking spot. I stood there listening to the wind and watching the sun starting to go down for sunset. It was an awesome view. Clay was right the roof top view makes you feel like you are on top of the world and closer to God. I zipped my coat for warmth. I closed my eyes and took in a deep breath.

Tears filled my eyes because I felt bad that I was being such a financial burden to the Thompsons. I knew that the restaurant meant a lot to Mr. Thompson. I did not know that Q's street gang went over to the restaurant and threaten Mr. Thompson again.

I did not want to go back to the abuse at home. I knew that if I continued to stay there, I feared that I would eventually become a drug addict and a prostitute just like mama.

Once I realized how Mr. Thompson felt about me, I knew that I could never again go to them for help. So I decided to take matters into my own hands, I was going to run away from home.

Suddenly I felt someone behind me and they place their hands over my eyes.

"Clay?" I smiled. I knew it was him from the scent of his cologne.

Clay sat down right next to me with a grin.

"What's with the gloomy face?" He looks at me with concern. He placed his hand upon my cheek and searched my face for answers.

"Clay, I can't take this anymore! I feel like I'm so alone and no one wants me." I started to break down into tears.

"Oh, Nia it's gonna be Ok."

"No Clay, it's not fuckin Ok!" I was so frustrated because it seem like no one fully understood my situation.

"Nia, calm down." Clay placed his hands upon my shoulders.

"How can I stay calm when my grandma is dead, my mother is a fuckin crackhead prostitute, and my stepfather is a fuckin gangster/drug dealer/pervert/ and pimp rolled up into one! And the Thompson's don't want me around anymore because I am too much of a burden!"

Clay reached over to comfort me.

"I don't have anyone to turn to and depend on. All of the adults involved in my life always let me down."

"What am I chopped liver? You got me." Clay hugged me. He reached into his Starters jacket and pulled out a tissue.

I dried my eyes and blew my nose.

"Ooh, girl I did not know you could hold so many buggers in that tiny nose." He frowned and touched my nose and then laughed.

Then I started to laugh too. Clay always had a way of making me laugh and feeling better.

"Ha, ha, ha, very funny."

"Nia, it looks like you are going to have to follow the other plan."

"What's that?"

"You can stay with my family."

"But, Clay…" He placed his index finger over my lips.

"I spoke to grandma and she already told me that she you could not stay."

"But why, Clay?" I became very disappointed.

"Grandma used to be a foster parent but since her health been failing with diabetes and losing her leg, she doesn't feel like she has the strength, especially now that she has me and my brother and sister to take care of."

I looked down and bit my bottom lips.

"Don't look so gloomy."

"The basement is the one place my grandma never goes to, so she would never know that you are there. Even my brother and sister don't go down there. The only way to get into the basement is through the back so I can give you a key. You can stay there until everything blows over."

"Thank you Clay." I leaned over and hugged him.

"No problem."

I took in a deep breath and closed my eyes in Clay's strong embrace.

Chapter#15

Betrayal

February 1987

I did not have any books for my classes at school because they were at my mama's house. My teachers were getting angry with me because I did not have any of them. I also needed my cloths, I only had five outfits to wear and I sometimes had to borrow some of Charlene's outfits to wear to school. I was too scared to go home but I knew that I had to go to mama's house to get my stuff.

Two weeks ago, I went to Hunts Point where mama goes to turn tricks. I could not find her. Q's street gang was often there selling drugs and pimping the prostitutes. I did see his gang out there so I knew that I could not stay out there too long to search for mama. It just was not safe.

Laporsha goes to my school and lived next door to my mom's house. Sometimes she would fill me in on what is going on with my mama when I was not there. She told me that she had heard that Q was in jail.

I spoke to Laporsha while at lunch.

"So girl, is Q really in jail?"

"Yeah, he is." Laporsha picked up her milk.

“So no one has been around the apartment?” I picked up my tray and followed her to the table.

“Nah it is safe. It should be ok to go by there,” said Laporsha.

“I guess I will swing by there then to get my stuff.

“When are you going by there?”

“I’m going to be there tomorrow after school. Can you and Rock go with me to get my things?”

“Sure, no problem.”

I approached the table where Charlene and Mary were sitting at. Charlene rolled her eyes at Laporsha. Laporsha gave a sly look at Charlene and then walked away.

I sat down at the table next to Charlene.

As soon as Laporsha walked away, Charlene started to talk.

“Girl, I do not like that girl! She is a snake!”

“Oh Charlene you never have liked her.”

“I don’t think you should go back there.”

“I’ll be fine. Laporsha and her big brother Rock will be going too.”

“Isn’t Rock a drug dealer?” asked Mary with a raised eyebrow.

“Yeah but, he is like a big brother to me. He has always looked out for me.”

“I would ask you all to come with me but I know you two are too scared to go into the projects.

“You damn right about that!” Charlene and Mary said it at the same time. They gave each a high five.

“Nia, we are just looking out for you. Be careful of Laporsha she is no good.” Charlene snapped her head with an attitude.

“Charlene’s right be careful, girl. I know you need to get your books and your cloths from over there. If I was you, I would just go in and then out.”

I listened to my two dearest friends but I needed to get the rest of my things out especially my school books. My teachers were getting on my case about not having my books and it was starting to show in my grades.

The next day I decided to go to mama’s house. Laporsha was not at school to go with me. She told me that it would be safe to go and get my stuff. So I decided to take her word and swing by after school.

When I went into the apartment, I opened the door. It was Q and two of his homeboys. They had on a baggy jeans and Addidas Sweatshirts. I quickly closed the door when I saw that they were there.

My heart was beating so fast. Q quickly opened the door.

"Where do you think you are going Baby Girl?" He yelled. Q's nostrils were flaring and he balled his fist. He had a gold ear ring in his ear and a large herringbone necklace around his neck. I was so scared.

He grabbed me by the arms and snatched me into the apartment. I tried to hold on to the door. I screamed at the top of my lungs. Q firmly coved my mouth. He was too strong he picked me up and brought me in. I was still kicking and swinging. I knew that he was going to do me a lot of harm. Q slapped me so hard that my lips started to bleed. My face began to sting.

"Hi, baby doll. Why are you trying to run away from your papa?" He gave me a perverted grin.

"I knew that you were going to come by the place sooner or later when you heard that I was in jail. I knew to just wait for yah."

His dark cold eyes stared into mines. He then ripped open my jacket and grabbed my breasts. He continued to fondle me. I tried to push his hands off of me. I turned my head away from him. My eyes were watery. I wanted to cry. He finally let me go.

There were two guys were separating the crack and cocaine in the back. They were putting them into plastic bags and packing them into boxes to be disturbed to local drug dealers. They both were carrying guns. This made me very nervous.

"Wow you are really starting to fill out. I need to take you back to the bedroom for old time sake. He stared at my breasts and licked his lips.

I crossed my arms across my chest.

I glanced over at Rock and he shook his head in disgust. Rock was over 6 feet 4 inches tall he was a dark chocolate complexion.

"Don't do that baby. I need to take you back to the bedroom and take advantage of that sweetness for old time sakes." Q reached over and forcefully pulled my arm away from my breasts. He started sexually assaulting me in front the two men that were in the room watching. I started crying.

“Hey man, you told Laporsha and me to get Nia over here. You did not say you were going to rape her.” Rock had a very concerned and angry look on his face.

“Look here, this is none of your business. Here is your money for both you and sister for bringing her here to me.” Q gritted his teeth and counted a couple of hundreds and gave it to Q.

I was so hurt and I looked at Rock with teary eyes. The look of betrayal was written all of my face.

“Now if you don’t like this then go outside and make sure no one suspicious is outside.”

Rock shook his head in guilt and left me.

After Rock left there was a knock on the door. And two more men came in. The men appeared to be in their late forties. They both were Italian. They were johns and they were Q’s best customers for his prostitutes. They wanted an extremely attractive young girl who has not been around.

“Well, well I see you have made it. I have a really good one here. She just turned sixteen and is has not hardly been around. She has the tightest pussy believe me I know. I have already given her a test run. Q ripped open my shirt and my bra was exposed. I tried to run but Q grabbed me and pulled a gun to my head.

“You run and I will fuckin kill both you and your mother.” He whispered into my ear.

Each john came around and looked at me like I was a piece of meat.

“I have to admit she is extremely beautiful. She is more stunning than you said she was.” I am willing to give $40,000 for her.”

“She is gorgeous; I will get her for 50,000.” Said Joey Torcelli, the other john.

“What about the $100,000 you said before?”

“She is not a virgin you said that you already took it so you will get less.”

“Damn it Anthony we had a deal!” Q balled up his fist.

“And look at her she is bleeding. You have been hurting this poor child.” Said Joey, the other john.

“Go clean your beautiful face sweet heart.” Joey rubbed my back and then grabbed my ass.

"Wow she has a very nice ass," said Joey. Joey and Anthony watched me lustfully go down the hall to the bathroom.

I went into the bathroom while in the front room they began to roar into a big argument. While Q and the two johns were arguing I was trying to plan my escape. I saw the window and saw that there was a fire escape. I opened the window and climbed out. Once I reached the bottom level, I ran as fast as I could.

While running I could hear Q yelling out of the window.

"Rock, get her. She is getting away!"

I buttoned up a few buttons to my shirt while I was running. Rock was right behind me. I ran around the corner and then tripped over a liquor bottle and fell. Rock caught me.

"Rock, please don't send me back," I pleated. I started to cry.

"Just hide inside this abandoned car and I will tell them I lost you ok." I inclined.

The other men came including Q.

"Where is she?" Q canvassed the area looking for me.

"She is gone she has gone to the subway." Rock covered for me.

"Damn it! She was our money ticket! We needed that money!" Q gritted his teeth.

They finally left. Once I felt that it was safe enough, I got out of the old beaten up car and headed to the subway.

Chapter #16

Hunts Point Red Light District

It was a Saturday night and Clay, Charlene, Mary, Greg, and Marcus, and I decided to go out. I really wanted to go see mama and see if she could bring me the rest of my belongings.

I spoke to my friends about going to see my mama. Clay didn't think it was safe for me to go alone, especially when I told him about what happened with Q. So everyone decided that we were going to go to Hunts Pointe Red Light District right before we go to the movies.

We all met up at the Thompson's restaurant. Once we left there we rode the subway to Hunts Pointe.

"I don't know if this was a good idea you guys. My parents are going to kill me. Why did I let you all talk me into this?" Charlene stated nervously.

"What happen to your sense of adventure?" I asked.

"Nia, I've never been to Hunts Point Red Light District. All I know is what I saw on TV." Charlene started to chew on her nails.

"Oh girl, we are in a group. I'm sure no one will mess with us," laughed Mary.

"Maybe I should tell your mama, Charlene," said Marcus with a raised eyebrow.

"Yeah Big Mouth Marcus, you can't keep a secret! I'm pretty sure you are good at getting other folks in trouble," said Mary.

"And any how your grandma is strict too. How are you going to tell on someone when she gives you butt whippings," said Greg jokingly.

"My grandma doesn't spank me," Marcus stuttered.

"Leave Marcus alone, he's just extremely honest and don't know how to lie," said Clay

"Thanks, man. Don't tell my grandma that I was out here!" Marcus was looking very nervous.

Everyone burst into laughter.

Finally we reached the red light district. The street walkers were definitely out and about looking for potential clients.

The street hookers were dressed in very provocative clothes, which left very little to the imagination. Even though it was fifty degree weather, the women of the night had on thongs, extremely short mini skirts, cleavage showing with extremely high heel shoes and boots.

A good looking prostitute approached the teenage boys.

"Hi sugar I can show you all a real good time." She rubbed Clay on the arms.

"No thank you."

One hooker had on a thong and had an extremely large butt.

"Damn did you see that?" Marcus tapped Clay on the arms.

"Yes I did." Clay stared at the attractive looking hooker. Greg was also checking her out.

I poked Clay to get his attention.

"Excuse me focus please! We are here to find my mother and not stare at the hookers."

An unattractive prostitute approached them. She looked like she was strung out on drugs. Her hair was nappy and some of her teeth were missing. "Hi, Baby, I am Ginger. Do you want some of this?" She started eyeing Marcus.

"Um no thank you." Marcus stuttered.

"You know that I love very young boys like yourself. I can tear you apart." The ugly prostitute started eyeing both Greg and Clay.

Clay and Greg look at her in disgust.

"Beat it lady! We are not interest." Clay dared her to solicit them again.

Then I finally spotted mama. Mama had on a red tight mini dress with high heals.

"Look there is my mama." I pointed my finger. We were about to approach her until we realize that Q's gang were near by. Q was lighting a cigarette. I was hoping that he would not look up because we were extremely close to where he was standing.

Unfortunately, he did look up and he spotted us from across the street. Q began to glare. Mama saw that Q spotted us and yelled, "Nia, run!"

"Shut up bitch!" He slapped Rachael across the face.

All of us started running. Clay took me by the hand and we ran as fast as we could.

Q signaled his gang to get us. "Get them!"

My heart was beating so fast.

Suddenly we all heard gun fire. One of Q's gang started firing at us.

Fortunately, we were close to the subway station.

The subway police was patrolling the area. The gang put away their guns.

We all hopped on the train within the nick of time. I looked out of the window and saw Q and the gang. They missed the trained. Q looked extremely outraged.

"Nia you almost got us killed! I am not going with you anymore to see your mama."

"Who were those people and why were they trying to kill us?" Clay asked.

I was still trying to catch my breath.

"That was Q, my stepfather. He is trying to get me into prostitution, as a sex slave. He's trying to sale me to this rich Italian mobster, name Joey Torcelli."

"Oh no, Nia, that is terrible," said Charlene.

Everyone sat down in silence as they thought about what just took place.

Chapter #17

The First Time

Journal Entry #62

Dear God,

Clay has been pressuring me into sex. I don't feel like I am ready. Now that I will be secretly staying with him, it is getting harder to say no. I am scared that if I don't give in to him that he will not let me stay there no more. Clay is my only peace and all I have in my life.

God, am I still a virgin or am I tossed goods even though my first sexual encounter was through rape? I am so confused, God. I hope that you still love me. I hope that you don't believe that it was my fought that my virginity was taken. My virginity was something that I really cherished and I wanted to save it for someone special. My prayer is for inner peace.

Love Always,
Nia

I took Clay up on his offer. I decided to move into his grandmother's basement. I felt bad because I knew that we were sneaking but I did not have no where else to go. I brought over a few of my belongings. Clay gave me a key.

"Here, Baby." He handed me the key and gave me a warm hug.

"Thanks Clay. I don't know what I would have done without you."

"No problem." Clay stared intensely into my eyes.

My heart started to beat really fast. Clay kissed me passionately with his soft full lips. He pulled me close; my soft breasts rest against his solid chest. His kissed me passionately with his soft lips. Clay caressed my juicy buns. His touch felt so good. Many thoughts began to race through my mind. I knew that we had to stop. I began to resist him. He pulled me back towards him. He continued to stroke my soft derrière. He reached over and started caressing my swollen breasts. He hands were underneath my blouse as he unsnapped my bra. He started to moan.

"Come on baby let's do it." He whispered in my ear.

"Clay, please stop I am not ready."

He ignored me and started caressing my bare breasts.

"You are so soft. You feel so good baby."

I moved his hands off my breasts.

"Clay, stop it!"

"Come on baby." He leaned over to try to kiss me again.

"I'm not ready." I turned my head.

Clay sighed in agitation.

"Ok fine!" he snapped. He left with out saying a word.

I watched him stormed out the door.

And hour later, Clay came back and we made back up.

Clay helped me get the studio apartment cleaned up. Even though my room was certainly not a luxurious place, I managed to call it home.

After dating each other for almost four months, Clay started pressuring me more about sex. One day, Clay and I were in basement chilling out after eating some Burger King. We moved from the table and sat down on the sofa bed to watch TV.

We enjoyed TV for about an hour, we watched "The Facts of Life" and "Different Strokes". Clay stared at me intensely. I had on a peach colored blouse and blue jean mini skirt to match. It was very warm inside so I took off my penny loafers and unbuttoned the first two buttons on my blouse.

I leaned back on my elbows and crossed my legs. Clay watched my every move. My eyes were still glued to the television.

Clay stared at the side of my face and my dimples showed every time I smiled or laughed. I looked up every once in a while and saw that he was still staring at me. When I caught him looking at me, I would smile at him.

Clay leaned over and kissed me on my cheeks and then passionately on the lips.

I playfully pushed Clay away from me and said, “Clay, come on now, I’m trying to watch TV.” I looked at him and smiled.

Clay leaned over and kissed me some more, but this time he placed his tongue in my mouth and gently intertwined it with mines. His hand moved down to my soft mounds; he gently squeezed and caressed them. I was scared. I was not ready for his advances, and I tried to push him away from me. His hands moved down to my butt.

He stopped kissing me on the lips and began to gently kiss me on the neck. It tickled at first I started giggling but then it started to feel really good. For the first time, I felt wetness within my most intimate spot. I knew we had to stop.

“Clay, please stop, I’m not ready yet.”

“Come on, baby, I’ll be gentle,” said Clay. His voice deepened.

His hand moved up my skirt; he gently caressed her soft thighs.

Suddenly, I had a flashback of Q raping me.

I started crying while Clay was on top of me.

“Get off me!” I yelled at him.

Clay grabbed my hands to keep me from hitting him.

“Nia, what’s wrong with you?”

I was so overwhelmed with fear that all I could do was cry.

“I’m sorry, Clay, but I can’t.”

Clay got up from the bed and turned off the TV set.

“Nia, I’ve been very patient with you! I’m starting to getting fed up with this!” Clay cursed.

“I’m sorry, Clay,” I apologized tearfully.

“Nia, it’s not like I haven’t been there for you. I’ve been nothing but good to you. All I’m asking from you is to love me back and to give me some every once in a while.”

Clay sat down next to me.

He reached over and placed his arms around me. He gently rubbed my back as I laid my head upon his shoulder. Clay reached in his pocket and pulled out a tissue.

“Here wipe your eyes.” I took the tissue and dried my tears.

Clay comforted me and continued to hold me gently in his strong arms. I felt so safe and warm that I almost fell asleep.

In a soothing voice, Clay said "Nia, making love is something special that is shared between two people, and that special something is what you and I share. I love you a lot, Nia. You're my baby, and I want this to be a beautiful experience that you will cherish for the rest of your life."

What Clay told me really touched my heart and I felt that what he said was truly sincere. I decided that I would go ahead and open up to him. I wanted to put my unfortunate rape experience behind me and move on with my life.

Clay leaned over and kissed me passionately on the lips, slowly unbuttoning my blouse. I was nervous. I wasn't sure if I should do this or not. My heart was fluttering.

Clay took off my bra. For a few minutes, he stared at my lovely honey colored breasts. He moaned as his strong hands began to caress my soft mounds. Slowly his hands moved underneath my skirt and caressed my soft firm inner thighs. His touch was so deliciously satisfying that I felt intoxicated with overwhelming passion and burning desires.

I could not believe that I was nude in front of a boy; this made me so nervous and shy. Clay stood up and took off his shirt. Enjoying his chiseled body I began I caressing his strong muscles and stroked his gorgeous six packs. Thrilled with the feel of his rock hard body, I stroked his strong broad shoulders.

"Clay you are so strong." I smiled at him nervously. He took off his blue jeans and underwear. After he finished undressing, he laid down beside me. I was scared when I saw his most intimate part. He grinned when he saw my reaction.

Clay got on top of me and kissed my entire body. The night air was filled with hot passion. His tender touch felt like paradise but in my mind I knew that it was wrong. A million thoughts were racing through my mind.

"Wait, Clay, I don't want to get pregnant! Maybe we should not be doing this."

Clay gently placed his finger over my soft lips and said, "Shh, shh, Baby I'm not going to get you pregnant. I'll put on a condom. It's going to be ok." He reached in his blue jeans pocket and pulled out a Trojan.

I remembered what Grandma Maria and Thelma taught me about waiting to have sex.

"Clay, it just doesn't feel right." I got up and put on my bra.

"Come on Baby don't do that."

"Clay, I don't want to do this."

"If you love me you would." Clay took my hand and stared at me intensely.

"Well if you love me we can wait. If we have a strong relationship, you will be there for me regardless." I pulled my hand away.

"Look Nia, I have needs. If we don't do this I will leave. Everyone in school is doing it."

"Why do we have to be like everyone else, Clay?"

"Look I'm leaving!" Clay put on his cloths and headed towards the door.

"Clay, please don't leave me. I don't have anyone else, I am all alone." My voice was shaking and my eyes were filled with tears.

Clay paused at the door. He came back and sat next to me. He put his arms around me in a warm embraced.

"You are not alone, Nia. I will be there for you."

I dozed off to sleep.

An hour later I woke up and Clay was still there. He woke up too when he felt me stir.

Clay leaned over and kissed with his soft full lips. Burst of passionate flames radiated amongst us as our tender bodies merged together as one. This time I gave in to his strong desires. We made love through out the night.

Chapter#18

Revealed Secrets

When I came home from Charlene's house, Clay was sitting on the sofa bed reading in my journal. I upset and outraged. He was so engrossed in my journal that that he did not realize that I had walked in.

"Clay, what are you doing?" I put my hands on my hip.

Clay jumped up so fast and closed my journal. He laid it down on the coffee table.

"Oh I did not know that you were going to be back so soon." Clay cleared his throat and scratched his head.

"Clay how could you? This journal is filled with my most intimate thoughts that I do not share with no one but God!"

Clay gave me a strange look. I could tell that he had already read too much of my journal. He knew my secrets.

"How long have you been reading my journal?"

"For about a week now," Clay glanced at me and then looked up at the ceiling.

"Clay! I did not want you reading my journal!" I grabbed my journal from the coffee table and held it closed to my chest.

"I'm sorry. It was it was laying on the table and it was so tempting."

I signed and glared at Clay.

"It's just that you are so secretive. And I can tell from your entries that you have gone through a lot. Why didn't you tell me that you were raped?" Clay's face was filled with concern.

"I did not want you to think any less of me." I looked down in shame.

"How can I think that way about you? It was not your fought, Nia." Clay got up and put his arms around me.

It felt so good to be in his arms. But I was still mad at him for reading in my journal.

"I still don't like you reading in my journal. What I write is between me and God." I punched him on the arm.

"Ouch! I guess I deserved that." Clay rubbed his arms.

"Yes you did!"

"I won't do that again."

"Good."

"So that rainy night when you first came to my house to spend the night was that when he had raped you?" He swept a strand of hair from my eyes.

"Yes it was."

"I thought so." Clay rubbed his fuzzy chin.

"Since we are sharing secrets, I want to know when you lost your virginity."

"Oh, I was fourteen years old in ninth grade."

"Really?'

"Yeah."

"So who was it?" I asked with a raised eyebrow.

"She was older. She was a senior at the time."

"Oh, I see."

"I have learned a lot from my older sexual counterparts." Clay gave a mischievous grinned.

I playfully punched him on the shoulder. "I'm sure you have. You're so nasty. How many girls have you slept with anyway?"

"Only three. You're my third."

"What about -," Clay placed his finger to my soft lips. He leaned over and kissed me.

"I know what we can do. Let's go and make out." Clay grinned.

"Nah, I think that you are on punishment for a minute. Let's play some Pac Man on your Atari."

“I’m down for that. But later on I want to play other things.” Clay hit me on my bottom and winked.

We spent the entire evening playing video games and we later made out.

Every night Clay came by to visit me in the basement. It was like a secret place of solitude for the both of us. We made passionate love each and every night.

One night, Clay came down to the basement to join me. He showed up at his usual time at 10:00 pm. He waits till everyone falls asleep before he comes down to see me and then each morning he would leave at 5:30 am. He did this to make sure he was back before everyone wakes up the next morning. But this time he was an hour late.

He finally arrived.

“I’m sorry I was late. I had to make sure grandma took her medicine and I had to tuck my brother and sister in. I finally got them to go off to sleep with a bedtime story.”

I was wearing Clay’s basketball jersey. His jersey was very loose on me so I wore it to bed like a night gown. Clay lent me his old basketball jersey since I did not have any cloths to wear for bed. I had just finished my algebra homework. He came over and kissed me on the lips. I then got up and started brushing my long soft wavy hair. I was about to twist my hair up into a ball.

“Don’t do that I like it when you have you hair down.”

Clay took my hair back down. My soft waves fell down upon my shoulders. Clay ran his fingers through my hair and stared intensely into my eyes.

Clay pulled me into his arms. He hand landed on my soft round buns. He gently squeezed my behind. His tongue rolled in my mouth. My heart was fluttering. He then swept me up and laid me on to the bed. He took off his clothes until the only thing he had on were his briefs. We stared at each other’s eyes. He laid next to me. We kissed each other in the heat of passion. He was about to enter me. Before we went any further I stopped Clay dead in his tracks.

“What’s wrong?” He asked.

“Do you have any condoms?”

“No I don’t. I ran out.”

“Well we can’t do it then.”

"Come on Nia I promise I will pull out."

"Clay, I'm scared I don't want to get pregnant."

"I promised I will pull out in time. Don't you trust me, Baby?"

I looked into his deep brown eyes, as he searched my beautiful face. I bit my lip as I was about to respond. He then kissed me. And with that he began to enter me. It felt so good but I knew that it was so wrong. For that moment in time my worries went away but this simple mistake was going to cost me in the long run. We rolled over relaxing in the after glow. We eventually fell asleep in each other's arms.

In the middle of the night, Clay began tossing and turning in his sleep. He woke up sweating and breathing really hard. He woke me up. Every since I had been sleeping over, I noticed that he always have nightmares around the same time every night, but he would never tell me what frightened him so much.

"Clay what is wrong?"

"I just had another nightmare. It is nothing. Just go back to sleep." Clay got up and went to the sink to get some water.

"Clay I know that something is wrong because you have this same nightmare almost every night around the same time."

Clay finished his glass of water and then laid back down.

Clay signed for a moment and then looked at me.

"Ok Nia, I am going to tell you what it is that has been bothering me. It is about my mom and dad. Do you remember when I told you about my mama being in jail and my father is dead?"

"Yes." I rolled over and cuddled up next to him.

"Well I am the cause of all of that."

"What do you mean, Clay?"

Clay's eyes were watery. I reached over and held his hands.

"My dad used to beat on my mother. Almost every night he went out and got drunk, he would come home and hurt mama for no reason. I love my mama so much and that I just got so sick and tired of my old man hurting mama. About two years ago, dad pulled a knife out on mom and was about to stab her. Before he could do it, I pulled out a gun and shot him dead. I was so filled with anger toward that man." Clay began to break down into tears.

"Oh, Clay I am so sorry to hear that." I hugged him and held him close. What he told me really touched me. I felt so sorry for him.

"My mom covered for me. She took the blame for murdering my father, because she did not want me to ruin the rest of my life by going to prison. My mom is in prison now for something that she did not do because of me. Right now I am filled with so much guilt."

"Baby, I did not know that you were going through all of this."

"You and your situation remind me so much of what my mother was going through. I just don't want anything bad to happen to you, Nia.

"I will be fine, Clay. I am right here. I am not going anywhere."

Now that his dark secret has been revealed to me, I felt more connected to him. Sharing our most intimate thoughts and feeling is what brought us closer together.

Chapter 19

Rumors

One day when I got to the studio apartment, Clay and Marcus were already there.

"Hi, Nia."

"Hi, Clay, how are you all doing?"

"I am doing fine. And I was about to get going." Marcus got up from the couch.

"Oh Clay are you going out with the fellas tonight?"

"Nah, I am going to hang out with my, girl."

"Oh well, I know what you all are going to do tonight!" Marcus gave an insinuating look as he walked out the door.

"Why did you tell Big Mouth Marcus our business?" I snapped. I was so furious that Clay told him.

"I don't know?" Clay shredded his shoulders.

"You know that he his going to tell everyone and it is will all over school. He always spreads rumors." I rolled my neck.

"Nia, Marcus is a close friend of minds."

"Yeah and every one knows that he has a big mouth!" I folded my arms.

"Come on Baby, you worry too much. You have a good reputation." He placed his hands on my shoulders.

"But I will not have a good rep if everyone knows that we are sleeping together. All of the boys will think that I am easy." My emotions were getting the best of me. I became teary eyed.

"Oh Baby everything is going to be OK. Marcus is not going to ruin your reputation." Clay reached over and hugged me.

"I hope so," I whispered under my breath.

A Week Later

All day at school the students were looking at me very strangely. I could feel people staring at me and pointing fingers. I could have sworn that they were talking about me. I felt so uncomfortable.

Lance the star football player approached me at my locker. Lance was a senior and he was extremely good looking. But he is also known for being a player.

"So Chavez how is it going?" He placed his hands on my shoulder and winked at me. His hands then moved down to my butt.

"Get your freaking hands off of me. I don't roll like that!" I snapped my head with an attitude.

"Come on, Baby. Let's go out sometimes. I can really show you a good time. Unlike your boyfriend, Clay." Lance gave me an insinuating look.

I rolled my eyes and gave him the brick wall. I walked away from him without saying another word.

Lunch Time

Lunch rolled around and Charlene sat down next to me.

"Hey, girl what is with the gloomy face?"

"People have been looking at me very strangely. I get the feeling that I am the topic of everyone's gossip." I began sipping on my carton of milk.

"Oh I had been meaning to tell you, Nia. There is a rumor going around school about you and Clay. I wanted tell you about it because I know that you would not be happy about it."

"What is it, Charlene?"

"Well, the word is that you and Clay are sleeping together. Now the boys think that you are easy. People are now saying that you are fast or a slut." Charlene spoke so fast that I had to sit and absorb all that she was saying. I was very upset and angry that my personal life was drawing so much attention.

"Charlene, who told you this?" I stopped sipping on my milk.

"Mary told me that she overheard people talking about you and Clay during homeroom. Is it true, Nia?"

"Yes, Charlene. I have slept with him but I did not want everyone to know."

"Really, why didn't you tell me? I am your BFF," said Charlene looking sad.

"I know Charlene, but we just started doing it about two months ago."

"Oh my, gosh! Girl, you are going to have to fill me in on every detail."

"I will but right now I don't like having my business out in the street. You know that I am a very private person." I swept my hair from my eyes.

"I know, Nia."

"Clay told big Mouth Marcus about us. And now everyone knows. Lance came on to me at my locker. That was when I knew that something was up. Lance only hits up on popular fast girls."

"Well, at least everyone knows that you exists, Nia."

"But not in a good way, Charlene. I really don't like this at all. To every one, I am now fast Nia, just like Miranda. I do not like having that type of reputation. Now all of the boys think that I am a whore and think that they can have their way with me."

"Maybe all of this will blow over, Nia."

"Girl, I hope so." I mumbled.

After school, I went to the basement apartment. I really wanted to talk to Clay about the bad rumors going around about me at school.

About thirty minutes later, Clay came home from school. He came in and sat next to me on the sofa.

"What's wrong?" He put his arms around my shoulders."

"I had a pretty bad day at school."

"Why?"

"Clay, Lance came on to me at school. He was rude and disrespectful. He started feeling on me. And people were constantly talking about me behind my back. The boys at school think that I'm a slut and don't respect me. I began to break down into tears."

"Nia, I'm sorry. It's not so bad." He rubbed my back. He leaned over to kiss me. I turned my head away.

"It's not so bad what do you mean it is not so bad? It's a double standard, if you have sex with a girl; you get high fives and everyone thinks highly of you. But when a girl does it she is called a whore or she is easy!" I got up from the couch.

"Why are you so angry at me?" Clay snapped.

"Why did you tell Big Mouth Marcus our secret? And now it is all over school! Now my reputation is being ruined by this! Why did you have to tell him?"

"I'm leaving! I'm not going to argue with you about this!" Clay stormed out of the apartment and slammed the door.

Later that night I dozed off to sleep. Lately I've been feeling exhausted. My period was late. I wanted to tell Clay but right now I was still angry about the negative rumor going around at school. I was at the point that I wanted to break off the relationship; I was literally an emotional wreck. Clay came over at his usual time, 10:00 P.M. He crawled into the bed next to me. He cuddled next to me and started caressing my breasts and kissing me.

"Clay, stop it. I'm tired."

"Come on Baby. I want some." Clay continued to grab my butt and caress my thighs.

"Clay, please not now!"

"You're still mad at me aren't you?"

"Yes I am. Better yet I think that we should call the relationship off." I snapped.

"What?" Clay had a hurt look on his face.

"You heard me. It is over!"

"Well fine then! I am leaving!" Clay storm out and slammed the door behind him.

Chapter # 20:

Street Ho

April 1987

Today was just not my day. It seemed like everything was not going my way. I saw Clay in the hall and he did not speak to me. Right during lunch, I saw Clay flirting with Sasha Davenport. He had his arms around her and was laughing. To make matters worse, Charlene and Mary sat down right next to me in the cafeteria when they saw Clay with another girl; which led to them wanting to know what led to our break up.

All three us of looked at Clay from across the cafeteria he was acting like I did not exist. I know that I told him that I wanted to break up with him because of the rumors. I was deeply hurt that he would replace me so soon. Obviously I meant very little to him for him to not even acknowledgement me through out the day. I was so upset that I walked out of the cafeteria in tears. I did not feel like explaining anything to Charlene and Mary all I wanted to do was to be alone and think. I went to the girl's bath room and sat in one of the stalls. I wasn't feeling too well. All of a sudden the burger I ate made me feel extremely nauseous and I started vomiting. I felt so clammy. I went to the sink and wiped my face off. I noticed that another month has past and I still did not have my period.

Lately I've been feeling more emotional than usual. I'm usually calm but all I seem to do is cry and want to be alone. The thought of Clay with Sasha made me burst into more tears. I thought about all of the times that Clay and I had sex together without protection. I was hoping that I was not pregnant. I remember when Laporsha told me about how she felt when she got pregnant last year. I knew that I was having some of the same symptoms. Maybe my period will come on later this month I hoped.

The bell rung it was time for me to go to math class. During math class, I was called to the office over the intercom. I only had ten minutes left before class was going to be dismissed. I was taken by surprise because I don't usually get called into the office unless it was something very important.

As I approached the front office, I saw my mama through the glass windows in the office. I was so embarrassed. I wanted to turn around and walk away but I didn't. Mama was dressed extremely provocatively. She had on a black spandex mini dress. Her mini dress barely covered her butt and her cleavage was showing. She had on a pair of red high stack pump with a three inch heels. Mama's hair hung loose with nappy spirals of red curls. It appeared that she tried to make her hair look a little bit better. It looked like she's been crying because her eyes were red and puffy.

The secretary at the front desk looked at mama distastefully. Mama saw that and started to cause a scene. "What the fuck you are looking at! Haven't you seen a street ho before! I charge $100 to do you and your man!" Mama rolled her eyes and put her hands on her hip.

The secretary look turned up her nose and looked at her in disgust. Mama laughed out loud at the secretary's reaction. There were some students in the office and they witnessed the entire scene. I saw them whispering. I knew that this was going to be all over school.

I tugged at my mama and gestured for her to leave the office. Mama finally calmed down. She had my overnight bag with all of my belongings in it.

"Hi mama what are you doing here?"

"Hi Nia, I had come to see you."

"Are you ok?"

"No, I'm not," Rachael folded her arms.

"What is it mama?"

"Nia, I'm sorry I came up here dressed in my street cloths but I had to rush and get your things." Rachael handed me my overnight bag.

"It's ok mama."

"Nia, can we go somewhere to talk? I really need to talk to you." Mama was shaking a little bit. I noticed that a couple of her front teeth were knock out of her mouth.

"Mama what happened to you?"

Mama and I went into a quiet room that was not used often in the school. I sat down and talked to mama.

"Baby, I have to leave and get away from Q I have witness some murders by his gang and the mob. And it ain't pretty. I don't want to become one of their victims. I am tired of being on the streets and I want to get myself cleaned up."

"Oh mom that is great!" I reached over and hugged her.

"I am going to rehab. I don't want Q to know where I am going."

"Do you need me to go with you?"

"No baby. I will be fine. I better get going before Q realized that I have gone missing. He is always watching me like a hawk. Especially since he knows that I know more about the ins and outs of their illegal activities."

"Did, Q threaten you mama?"

"Yes, he has. He told me that if I leave that I will surely die. That is why I must get out of town." Mama stood up and gave me a hug.

"I love you mama."

"I love you too." Mama shivered and rubbed her arms. She did not look to well. I watched mama walk down the hall. Some students stared at her and snickered as she walked out the door. I went to the window and stared at mama as she gradually disappeared into the distance.

Chapter #21:

Lover's Spat

Last night Clay did not visit me in the basement. I slept in the bed all alone. I really missed him. I knew that Clay was mad at me. I hoped that he did not tell his grandma that I was living in the basement. When I went to school, I saw Clay with Sasha again. This time he was talking with her at the locker. He looked at me and watched me as I walked past him.

I went to my locker. Roderick Hernandez, captain of the football team approached me. He was so tall and handsome and so very popular.

"Yo Nia, what's up?" Roderick stared intensely into my eyes.

"Fine." I smiled. I could not believe that Roderick was talking to me. I was somewhat happy but wondered why all of sudden he had an interest in me when at first he literally did not know that I existed.

He gently caressed my shoulder with his fingers. I did not like that so I moved away.

"I want yah to kick it with me at the Da Party at Jesse's house this Friday night." He leans towards me and grinned. His mouth was filled with gold.

I really was not interested in Roderick because he was not my type. He was a light skinned biracial guy part black and Puerto Rican, just like me, but I tend to prefer dark chocolate. Plus he was so conceded and thuggish. I was about to turn him down but I saw Clay waiting for class across the hall so I said loudly so that he could hear. "Why sure Roderick I would love to go with you to the party."

"Well here's my number call me sometimes." Roderick winked.

I smiled and then glanced over at Clay. Clay looked annoyed and walked into his class.

Right after school when I got to the apartment Clay was already there.

"Hi, I am surprise to see that you are already here." I closed the door.

"What was all that about with you and Roderick!" Clay got up from the couch.

"I am going out with him this Friday." I grinned.

"Nia, I don't think that is a good idea!" He approached me.

"Why not, Clay? I saw you and Sasha all lubby dubby in the cafeteria yesterday!" I rolled my head.

"Didn't you just break up with me?"

"Well yes. But I did not think that you would move on so fast."

"See you take me for granted. And I have needs Nia. I move on when I don't get it. But let's get off the topic of me and about you going out with Roderick." Clay folded his arms and then rubbed his chin.

"What about it?"

"Please, Nia don't go out with him. I over heard him talking about you in gym class today to some guys. I was about to kick his ass but some of my friends had to literally get me off of him!" He balled his fist. I noticed the angry look on his face.

"Really what happen?"

"Roderick said that you was a street ho just like your mama and since you slept with me that you was an easy lay. He was skimming with his friends on how they were going to gang rape you at the party."

"Oh Clay I did not know that. Thanks for sticking up for me. I didn't know that you still care about me."

"Yes I do." He grinned.

"But what about you and Sasha?"

"There is no me and Sasha. I just did it to make you jealous. I asked Sasha to pretend to be flirting with me in the cafeteria. I wanted to teach your ass a lesson for breaking up with me."

"Well it worked I was very pissed off at you. And I was not interested in Roderick. I was just using him to get back at you."

"I knew it! He is not even your type. You like chocolate brothers just like me. I am milk chocolate just like you like it." He grinned and rubbed his chin.

"I knew that you were mad though. I could feel you watching me as I was talking with him."

"Yes, and it took a lot for me to restrain myself. I wanted to kick that niggas ass. You know that Roderick is my arch rival. He's always trying to steal my girlfriend. When he found out that we had broken up he wasted no times trying to hit up on you." Clay placed his arms around my waist.

"I am sorry boo. I did not mean to hurt you. I should have not broken up with you over a rumor." I reached over and hugged him.

"I'm sorry too, baby." Clay leaned over and kissed me passionately on the lips. We continued to hug each other in a warm embrace. We promised each other not to let trivial things come between us.

Chapter #22:

Q's Revenge

May 1987

On a sunny Saturday morning I ran into Laporsha at my job. I was still working at a local grocery store as a store clerk. Laporsha came into the store to pick up some formula for her baby.

"Hi, girl! I see that you are still working here at the store."

"Yeah I have been working here for about six months now."

"Wow, time really goes by fast. I remember when you first started working here. I am glad we had a chance to run into each other. There is something important that I need to talk to you about, Nia."

"Oh, really." I was really skeptical of Laporsha especially when she and her brother betrayed my trust. I was hesitant to talk to her.

"Nia, I am so sorry about what had happened with Q. He lied to us and told us that your mama was looking for you. He did not tell us that he was trying to hurt you."

"Ok, I get off in about another ten minutes. I can talk to you on the way to the substation." I glanced down at my watch.

"Ok, Nia."

Towards the end of my shift I had to finish stocking shelves. I was in deep thought as I thought about the home pregnancy test I took yesterday. The test was positive. I was so scared. I didn't wanted to go to the clinic to see a doctor but I knew that I needed go because I wasn't feeling well. Sometimes I had real bad pelvic pains that I have not felt before. I wanted to ask Laporsha some questions because she was pregnant last year. I finished stocking the last can goods from the crate. I was contemplating as to how I was going to ask Laporsha without her knowing my situation.

I left the store and met Laporsha out front. I wanted to ask her about which clinic she went to when she was pregnant.

"So Laporsha what's up?"

"I'm fine. Alisha has been keeping me up all night. I had to I picked up her some more formula before she runs out." Laporsha got up from the bench.

"Do you ever hear from her father, Brian?"

"Not too often. He is such a jerk; he left me when he went off to college. And I am pretty much stuck trying to raise Alisha by myself. Formula is so expensive. I had to get on the WIC Program."

"I am so sorry Laporsha. I thought Brian was a nice guy."

"Well he's not." Laporsha rolled her eyes.

"Laporsha which clinic did you go to when you was pregnant?"

"Oh I went to the teen center on 24th Street."

"Why?" Laporsha had a crossed look on her face.

"Oh it is nothing." I shrugged my shoulders

"So what did you have to tell me Laporsha?" We were at the subway station.

"Oh yeah, my brother, Rock, wanted me to relay a message to you." We both boarded a train and then sat down.

"What is the message?"

Laporsha sighed as she put her bag of groceries down.

"Q is looking for you. Because A. he is trying to track down your mother because she knows too much information and he does not want it to get to the police. And B. he wants to sell you as a sex slave to a mob boss. He is literally trying to hunt you down," whispered Laporsha.

"What?"

"Nia, I really came to the grocery store to let you know what is going down the pipe."

"You may want to consider moving to another school and going into hiding like your mother.

"When did this happened?"

"Last night. So try to avoid Q's hotspots. And try to lay low."

"Thanks Laporsha. "

"No problem, girl. Well this is my stop. Be careful Nia. Q is someone you don't want to play with." Laporsha had a worried look on her face.

"Don't worry, girl. I will be just fine."

"Ok then see you later," Laporsha waved and stepped off the subway and I waved back.

What Laporsha told me had me deeply disturb. I took heed to Laporsha's warnings.

Three days later

I went to the teen clinic on 24th Street. One of the nurses gave me a free pregnancy test. After they took my urine sample, I prayed that the test would come back negative. I was not ready to be a mama. *God please let this test come back negative*. I was so scared because I knew that I had no the money or the means to raise a child. The fifteen minutes of waiting seemed like and eternity. The nurse came back with my results.

"Ok dear, you are pregnant." I was in denial at first. I did not want to believe that I was actually pregnant. I broke down into tears because I did know what I was going to do and how I was going to tell Clay. I just did not know how he was going to react when I tell him the news.

The nurse placed her hand on my shoulder. "It is going to be Ok honey. Here's some tissue."

I took the tissue and dried my eyes.

"We do have a counselor that you can speak to. Do you need to see one?" The nurse looked over my charts.

"No thank you." All I wanted to was to leave and go somewhere alone to think.

"Ok well here is a card to our counselors just in case you change your mine. And here are some extra resources that you can read."

I left the center in dismay. I went to our secret spot, the rooftop. I sat down to be alone. I looked up at the sky. The clouds were so beautiful in the sky and I could feel a gentle breeze. A sense of peace came over me. I could see how Clay say that the roof top makes you feel closer to God. I closed my eyes and I began to pray.

Friday Night

I told Clay about Laporsha's warning about Q But Clay still wanted to go out with all our friends to the movies. He insisted we can still go out to the movies just for old time's sake.

On a Friday evening of May 1988, I had a bad feeling about us going out to the movies.

"Nia we have been coupled up in this basement all week and I just want for us to go and have a good time."

I really wanted to go catch a movie too. I have not seen Q around and I have made sure I avoided his hang out spots. So I figured if we go further out to Brooklyn that we should be ok from harm.

I had a worried look on my face and we were getting ready to leave.

"Come on, Baby, you have nothing to worry about. You look so worried." And with that, he smiled and gave me a big hug. He gently ran his fingers through my soft hair and looked into my beautiful brown eyes.

I looked away from him for a moment. I had a lot on my mind. I had been to the clinic that day and found out I was pregnant. In a way, I was hesitant to tell Clay.

"What's the matter, baby?"

"Clay, it's just that I have something to tell you."

"Aw, Baby, can't this wait? We are going to be late meeting our friends at the movie theater." asked Clay hastily.

"Well, I guess it could wait."

"OK, then we'll be back in a few hours. Now, Baby, you need to take that sad look off your face, we are going to be fine. Q is not going to hurt you and plus we will be in a group."

He placed his arms around my waist and said, "Now give your Big Daddy a smile." I finally smiled and laughed at Clay's silly expression on his face.

"Good Baby, now that's what I like to see, that pretty smile of yours."

Clay leaned towards me place a soft loving kiss upon my lips. His hands slowly lowered down to my butt and with that he whispered in her ear, "You know what we're going to do when I get back. We're going to get busy tonight."

I smiled and tip toed to place a sweet kiss on his cheek. Clay's deep, dark, dreamy looking eyes stared right into mines.

"I love you, Nia."

"And I love you too."

Four hours later, we left from the movie theater and had dinner with the crew (Charlene, Mary, Marcus and Greg). We saw "Nightmare on Elms Street Part 4: The Dream Master." After dinner we all went our separate ways. Clay and I headed back to his house.

"That movie was off the chain!" said Clay.

"It made me scared."

"I know I saw you flinching over there. You are so scary." We got off the subway and headed home.

"I can't believe that I let you guys talk me seeing that movie. I hate horror films." I looked and saw heard a car with screeching wheels. I looked up and saw Q's car along with two other cars.

"Oh my God! Clay, run!

"We ran as fast as we could up the street. We went up a dark alley.

The car drove past the alley.

"Nia you go on while I go the other way!"

"No Clay I want to stay with you!"

"They are really after you. You keep going so that you can getaway and I will throw them off your trail by going the oppositedirection. I will meet you at our secret spot ok."

Clay kissed me on the lips.

I kept on running down the alley to another side street. I got away.

In the distance I heard gun shots. "Bang, Bang!" And then I heard police sirens.

I ran back to see what happened. Around the corner, I saw Clay lying on the ground.

I screamed, “Clay! Oh my God, no!”

I kneeled down by his side and told him that everything was going to be all right. I was thankful that he was still alive.

Clay’s shirt was soaked in blood.

He looked at me and tried to talk, “I’m cold.”

I took off my coat and wrapped it around him. I looked down at him and saw that he was continuing to bleed very heavily. Luckily the police was not too far. When the police heard the gun fire they went to check it out. Q and his gang fled the scene when they saw the police coming.

Teary eyed I told him, “Baby you will be all right. I love you so very much and I don’t want you to die.”

Clay looked up at me and smiled and began to cough heavily.

“I love you, too, Nia. I know that sometimes I don’t show it and say it, but I really do.”

I gently wiped tears from Clay’s eyes. Seeing him in this condition hurt me deeply; I wanted so badly to take the pain away.

“Nia, I want you to have my silver jeep that I was planning on fixing up one day,” whispered Clay.

“Clay, please don’t talk that way. Baby, you’re going to make it. You have to because I found out that I am pregnant when I went to the clinic today, and that’s what I wanted to tell you earlier.”

Clay smiled at me, “If it’s a boy will you name him Clay Jr.?”

“Why, of course, I will,” I sobbed.

“Nia, the baby is going to be a boy,” whispered Clay.

“Shh, shh, you need to rest. I know it hurts when you talk, because the pain is written all over your face,” I said softly as I placed my finger upon his lips.

I continued to hold Clay in my arms and tried to keep his trembling cold body warm.

Clay began to wince in pain. The ambulance arrived few minutes later. I kissed Clay on the lips and told him that everything was going to be fine. I held his hands and his hands were trembling. Clay was rushed to the hospital.

After reaching the hospital, Clay was rushed to emergency surgery. His uncle came when he heard that his nephew had been shot.

About four hours after Clay was taken into surgery, the doctors finished and sent him to the intensive care unit.

I was relieved that Clay survived his gun shot wounds.

A week later, Clay was still at Southview Health Center recovering from his gun shot wounds to his arm and shoulder. I went to the hospital to see him.

I strolled into Clay's room. Clay was sitting up watching TV. He smiled when I approached him.

"Hi, Baby."

"Hi, Clay, we need to talk." I gave Clay a hug

"Yeah, I agree."

I sat down in a chair next his bed.

"Is your uncle here?"

"No he's at work. Now we can talk about our situation." Clay gestured for me to sit next to him on his bed.

"Nia, I'm not ready to be a father." Clay placed his hand on my lap.

"I don't want to be a mom either; I can barely take care of myself. I'm so scared, Clay." I held his hand. Tear filled my eyes.

"How far along are you?" Clay placed his hand on my belly.

"The doctor told me almost three months." I bit my bottom lip.

"He reached over and held my hand in his. I leaned over and gave him a hug.

I felt so safe in his warm embrace.

“The good news is that Q was arrested. The police locked him up and some of his street gang in jail. Now I don’t have to worry about him finding me.”

“I am glad that motherfucker is behind bars,” Clay’s nostrils flared as he balled up his fist in anger.

“I don’t know what we are going to do, Clay.” Clay got some Kleenex and gently wiped my face.

He ran his finger through my long soft hair. I turned my head and we kissed each other on the lips.

“Don’t worry about it we are going to make it. We will figure this out when I get out of the hospital.”

We both sat in silence as we both thought about our tragedy. We held each other in a strong embrace as we worried about problems that were beyond our age of innocence.

Want to find out what happens next? Get the second book to the
Purpose Lies Within - Nia Trilogy Novel Series,
Weathering the Storm.

About Kimberly Purpoz

Kimberly Purpoz has been a professional writer and author for over 12 years. Ware launched Messenger Publishing, Inc. in 1998. Kimberly Purpoz is an author of several books under her current name and her previous pen names, Kimberly S. Phillips and Kimberly Ware. Kimberly writes under the following pseudonyms: Kimberly Purpoz and Purpoz. She has written several books and coauthored one book. The following are the titles of her books: “The Nia Trilogy”, “How to Release the Book in You” co-authored with Dr. Johnnie Swanson, “Heal My Wings: A Healing Guide for Women” and “Heal My Wings: A Healing Journal and Workbook for Women.”

Kimberly is also the writer and creator of the upcoming teen book series “Candace Green Mystery Series”. She is currently working on the first book to her new paranormal novel series called *Foreshadowers*.

Kimberly also writes for Associated Content and the Examiner. Kimberly lives in Decatur, Georgia with her family.

Her email address is: authorpurpoz@yahoo.com
Website: http://www.kimberlypurpoz.com
Wiki: http://www.purpoz.wetpaint.com

www.ingramcontent.com/pod-product-compliance
Lightning Source LLC
LaVergne TN
LVHW090959080826
845145LV00003B/1059

* 9 7 8 0 9 6 6 7 9 1 3 9 6 *